"Hang on, Hayley" Cain yelled.

Hayley fell back from the flames that were crawling closer to her. A few moments later Cain was back. She heard a fire extinguisher and then could see him in the flames coming toward her. Big, strong, capable.

He yanked her into his arms. "Are you okay?"

She nodded.

"Stay close to me. We've got to move fast. Keep low."

He pulled her in front of him, wrapping his body protectively around hers, using the extinguisher he held in front of her to make a path for them. Cain pulled her through the front door, both desperately sucking in oxygen as they hit clean air.

"Are you okay?" he asked again once they could breathe, watching the fire trucks roll in.

"Yes." Her voice sounded rusty. Hoarse. But already her lungs were easing.

He yanked her into his arms again, cradling her head against his chest.

That had been way too close.

MAJOR CRIMES

USA TODAY Bestselling Author
JANIE CROUCH

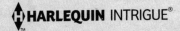
HARLEQUIN INTRIGUE®

This book is dedicated to Hayley, aka Mandy. How blessed I am to still have you in my life all these years later. We may be continents apart (I move to one…you move to another) but I treasure your friendship and the memories we have. To Mandy, love Mittie. xx

ISBN-13: 978-1-335-52649-6

Major Crimes

Copyright © 2018 by Janie Crouch

Recycling programs for this product may not exist in your area.

Printed in U.S.A.

www.Harlequin.com

Janie Crouch has loved to read romance her whole life. This *USA TODAY* bestselling author cut her teeth on Harlequin Romance novels as a preteen, then moved on to a passion for romantic suspense as an adult. Janie lives with her husband and four children overseas. She enjoys traveling, long-distance running, movie watching, knitting and adventure/obstacle racing. You can find out more about her at janiecrouch.com.

Books by Janie Crouch

Harlequin Intrigue

Omega Sector: Under Siege

Daddy Defender
Protector's Instinct
Cease Fire
Major Crimes

Omega Sector: Critical Response

Special Forces Savior
Fully Committed
Armored Attraction
Man of Action
Overwhelming Force
Battle Tested

Omega Sector

Infiltration
Countermeasures
Untraceable
Leverage

Primal Instinct

Visit the Author Profile page at Harlequin.com.

CAST OF CHARACTERS

Cain Bennett—Head of the Omega Sector protection and recovery division. Tasked with discovering the traitor inside Omega Sector.

Hayley Green—Computer expert and Cain's high school sweetheart. Just getting out of prison for computer fraud, having been sent there by Cain.

Steve Drackett—Director of the Omega Sector critical response division.

Ren McClement—Omega Sector founding agent with highest levels of security clearance.

Mason Green—Hayley's three-year-old son.

Ariel Green—Hayley's cousin.

Timothy Smittle—Hayley's boss at the Bluewater Grill, where she works.

Mara—Waitress and Hayley's friend at the Bluewater Grill.

Damien Freihof—Terrorist mastermind determined to bring down Omega Sector piece by piece by doing what they did to him: destroying their loved ones.

"Fawkes"—Omega Sector traitor providing inside information to Freihof.

Lillian Muir—Omega Sector critical response division SWAT team member.

Senator Ralph Nelligar—US senator leading the charge to crack down on computer crimes.

Joshua Lawson—Assistant to Senator Nelligar.

Omega Sector—A multiorganizational law enforcement task force made up of the best agents the country has to offer.

Prologue

Omega Sector agent Cain Bennett sat in the back row of a Georgia courthouse waiting for the judge to come in and sentence the woman Cain had loved since he was sixteen years old.

Hayley Green, the woman Cain had arrested.

He scrubbed a hand over his face, then leaned forward to rest the weight of his forearms on his knees. Hayley currently sat ramrod straight at the table directly in front of the judge's bench, in a Fulton County orange jumpsuit, her straight blond hair in a ponytail behind her. She was obviously ignoring the whispers from the crowd that was here to see her sentenced. Press, government figures, even some people from their small Georgia hometown who wanted to be able to report the gossip live filled the room.

You would think she was about to be sentenced for murder rather than computer hacking.

He still hadn't figured out why Hayley chose to use her ninja-like computer skills illegally, to hack the College Entrance Test—CET—system. The exam, which allowed students to get their results back instantly rather than having to wait months like previous standardized tests, was supposed to be un-hackable. Questions completely random.

Hayley and her cohorts had figured out not how to hack the test, but how to build false exams into the system. Ones that the system thought were real and that gave the students who "took" them real scores and credit.

Rich students were willing to pay handsomely for these false exams and scores, which would, in essence, assure their acceptance into any college they desired. A pretty nifty scam when it was all said and done. But why she had done it, Cain had no idea. The girl he'd known in high school would never have.

And Hayley sure as hell wasn't going to offer any reasons why to Cain. She was refusing to talk to him at all.

He gritted his teeth in a constant tension he'd lived with for the past several months. Yes, he'd reignited his relationship with Hayley because of the hack-ing case.

But because he'd thought she might be able to put him in contact with some of the hackers, not because he thought *she* was one of them.

But to her it just looked like he'd slept with her as part of some damn sting operation.

Cain looked up at Hayley's still, stiff form in the chair. God, he'd made a mess of things. She had, too. Why the hell had she been hacking? Become a criminal? She knew he'd dedicated his life to law enforcement. Choosing to break the law was like a slap in the face after what they'd once shared.

But hopefully the judge would take into consideration that Hayley had no prior convictions, no arrests. She'd pleaded no contest in order to not drag out the case and cost taxpayers thousands of dollars in a trial. Cain, as the agent who had been in charge of the investigation, had petitioned for no jail time for Hayley.

Parole with limited computer usage, definitely. But Hayley wasn't dangerous. Had no intent to harm others. Time already served would be a perfect sentence for her.

She might not like it, but Cain planned to be a lot more present in her life. He'd been wrong to let them grow so far apart as he'd gone to college, then the FBI training academy, before joining Omega Sector. They'd talked via social media and email, but he obviously had not been privy to what was really going on in her life. Aka: criminal activities.

That would stop now.

The judge would release her today, and tomorrow Cain would begin to bulldoze his way back into her life. She'd be mad—hell, so was he—but they would work through it. They had too much history, too much passion, too much *rightness* to be without each other for long. Hayley Green was his, the same way he was hers. They had been for over ten years.

Beginning tomorrow, he was going to make sure his little felon had her own law enforcement agent keeping her on the straight and narrow. Cain smiled slightly. It wouldn't be easy, but she was worth it. *They* were worth it.

The bailiff announced for all to rise as the judge entered the courtroom. Everyone sat back down as the judge asked Hayley to stand.

Cain listened as the judge spoke to Hayley about computer crimes, although not violent, not being victimless. He grew more tense as the judge pointed out that she'd stolen not just from the company that developed and ran the CET, but from students around the country who had missed out on the opportunity of college acceptance and scholarship because of the test results she had sold for money.

Bile began to burn at the back of his throat when the judge said that Hayley had not just hacked computers, she had stolen futures.

This was not good.

"Today," the judge continued, "I feel that it is important to set an example. To show that people like you, Ms. Green—young, intelligent, able to work— will be held to strict standards when you choose to break the law. To discourage others from making the same choices."

Cain wanted to stand up. Stop time. Do *something*. Because the next words to come out of the judge's mouth were going to alter Cain's entire world.

He couldn't imagine what they were going to do to Hayley's.

"Hayley Green, you have pleaded nolo contendere to a charge of first-degree computer crimes, which is a class B felony, with a sentence of up to twenty years in prison. This court hereby sentences you to ten years at the Georgia Women's Correctional Institution, Minimum Security Campus, eligible for parole not before four years."

Cain saw Hayley's body jerk as the gavel came down against the sound block on the judge's bench. The judge said a few more things and then court was dismissed.

Cain couldn't believe what he'd just heard. Feeling like all the oxygen had been sucked from the room, he stared at Hayley, still standing stiffly at the table as her lawyer murmured something in her ear. Hayley's cousin Ariel, the only family present, was crying softly in the row behind her.

Four years. Hayley would spend at least four years in prison.

And Cain had sent her there.

People began filing out around him, but Cain couldn't force himself to move. Couldn't stop looking at Hayley. Couldn't figure out how to make this right.

Things would never be right again.

An officer came over to her and asked her to move to the other side of the table so he could handcuff her. She did, moving slowly, like she was in shock. Which she had to be.

Four years.

As the officer turned her so he could cuff her, Hayley's eyes met Cain's. He took a step toward her, unable to help himself.

He expected tears, or terror, or even hatred to light her eyes as she looked at him, skin across her cheekbones pale and drawn.

But her eyes were dead, emotionless. She looked at him as though he were a stranger.

Then she turned from him completely and was led away.

Chapter One

Four years later

Cain often dealt with the worst of humanity as part of the Omega Sector Protection and Recovery Division.

Crisis management and bodyguarding were a regular part of his job. He and his team also dealt with hijackers and kidnappers on a regular basis.

But his mission right now was to rescue not a person, but the entire Critical Response Division of Omega, which was being hijacked in its own way.

They had a psychopath on their hands, set on destroying the team one by one—by killing their loved ones. And someone on the inside was helping the madman in his quest.

Cain was currently watching a video of Damien Freihof—said psychopath—who had slit the throat of Omega psychiatrist Grace Parker last week.

Freihof and his cohort within Omega Sector had decided it would be fun to send the murder as a live feed to all active Omega Sector agents—forcing them to watch as Dr. Parker died without them being able to step in and do anything about it.

So now Cain was able to watch it over and over. Watch as Grace's eyes dulled in death. Watch as Freihof's eyes had filled with something akin to joy as the doctor—a beautiful woman in her fifties, and an integral part of the Omega team—died sitting right in front of him.

Freihof had made it no secret that he wanted Omega Sector's Critical Response Division to pay for the death of his wife, Natalie, years ago. That he blamed the elite law enforcement task group for her untimely demise in a bank hostage situation.

He was determined they would feel the pain of losing loved ones like he had.

Grace Parker had been just one of those loved ones Freihof had gone after. For the past five months he'd been the mastermind behind attacks on nearly a dozen Omega Sector agents or their friends and family. Grace had died last week. Two other Omega agents were in the hospital after an explosion.

And Freihof was reveling in it all.

Freihof had to be stopped. But just as importantly, the mole inside Omega—the one who was feeding Freihof information that was allowing him to be so successful in his attacks—had to be stopped. Steve Drackett, director of the Critical Response team, was unsure who could be trusted.

That's why Cain was here, brought from a different division of Omega, to help catch this traitor.

Cain watched the death of Grace Parker again, hoping to notice something this time that maybe he'd missed before. He hadn't personally known the woman, which allowed him to look at the footage more objectively, see things others—people who had cared deeply about the psychiatrist—might miss.

Cain was known for his ability to separate emotion from the job. It was how he'd risen to assistant director of Omega's Protection and Recovery Division when he'd barely reached his thirtieth birthday.

Because he got the job done, no matter what.

He'd proven that four years ago.

Cain studied the footage again, pushing all thoughts of Hayley Green aside. Right now he needed to understand as much as he could about Damien Freihof. Because anything Cain could find out about him would hopefully lead to information about the mole.

In a way—as psychotic as Freihof was—he was easier to understand. The man wanted vengeance. Sure, he may want vengeance for something that Omega Sector wasn't actually responsible for, but at least his motives were clear.

What did the traitor want?

There couldn't be much money involved in helping Freihof. Maybe a little, but not the sort of big payoff someone was usually looking for in order to risk their reputation and/or life.

That left a lot of other factors. It could also be vengeance; maybe Freihof had found a kindred spirit also looking for some sort of revenge for something Omega had done. Maybe the person had a desire for control, or was some sort of political zealot, planning to bring down Omega Sector from the beginning.

Or maybe Freihof had control over the man—or woman—and was blackmailing him or her in some way.

The motive didn't really matter to Cain in terms of justifying why the traitor was behaving the way he was, but understanding motive always provided information in an unknown suspect.

Cain sat in a private conference room attached to Steve Drackett's office. It was one of the few places Steve had assured him there was no way the mole could have any type of surveillance devices.

While Cain trusted Steve completely, he wasn't leaving anything to chance. Cain had his own counter-surveillance device that allowed him to know for certain that no one was recording or transmitting visual or audio data from this room.

Files of every employee—agent or not—of the Critical Response Division sat in groups on the large conference table. Cain had already been in this room for more than eight hours going through the files.

He had four distinct groups: cleared, unlikely, unknown and suspicious.

People like Steve Drackett, whom Cain had known for years and who had spent most of his life fighting people like Freihof, were in the cleared category. Other agents also, like the various members of the Omega SWAT team who had been injured or nearly killed by Freihof over the last few months. Employees who had joined Omega very recently were also cleared, as well as those who had no access to the type of information that had been given to Freihof.

But that still left a hell of a lot of people in the unlikely, unknown or suspicious categories.

Long-term operatives and agents were in the unlikely category. Cain rubbed the back of his neck as he walked around the table looking at the files. The thought of the culprit being a colleague who had been involved with Omega Sector for years churned like acid in his gut. He drowned those thoughts by taking a swig from his now-cold coffee mug, the only substance he'd had today. He wanted to move these agents to the cleared list, but he couldn't.

Emotion had no place in solving crimes. No matter how much Cain wanted someone to be innocent, he knew firsthand that wasn't always how things panned out.

He looked through all the unknown files again. People with a background in computers who would be able to get Freihof the information he wanted without being detected. The one thing they knew for sure was the traitor was highly skilled in computer usage.

But a number of people were skilled in that area. Even people who had jobs not involving computers or intel could still have the prowess needed to be the mole.

Cain picked up a file for John Carnell. The guy was a genius; his damn mind worked like a computer. Abrupt and sullen, he was often difficult to work with, but almost always the smartest person in the room.

Cain slid Carnell's file from the unknown to the suspicious pile. There it joined half a dozen others. Two from people who had filed complaints with the head Omega office in Washington, DC, when they were bypassed for promotions—maybe one of them had an ax to grind and had become the mole. SWAT wannabe Saul Poniard's file was also in the pile; he had such a perfect record that it bugged Cain.

And Lillian Muir, a member of the SWAT team. Cain didn't like putting her name in the suspicious pile, especially since she'd been one of the people injured in an explosion a few days ago at Freihof's last known place of residence. A wooden projectile had lodged itself in her shoulder. A painful but non-life-threatening injury.

But Cain could not deny that Lillian's past—and how well hidden she'd kept it—made her a suspect. Someone who had gone to the lengths she had to hide her past was someone who had something to lose.

When Steve Drackett walked in the door, Cain slid Lillian's file under another one. He knew Steve was too emotionally involved with his inner team to objectively consider the possibility that one of them was the traitor.

"How's it going in here?" Steve asked.

"I'll admit, I'd rather be out enjoying your beautiful Colorado mountains than stuck inside this windowless room."

Steve clapped him on the shoulder. "I keep saying you need to transfer from the DC office out here. Quality-of-life clause." Steve's eyes flew to the screen where Cain had paused the recording of Grace Parker's death.

Cain walked over and shut it off. Steve had seen the murder footage enough times; he didn't need to see it again. Steve gestured toward the files on the table. "Any luck?"

"I have my theories. My categories of suspects. I have to be honest with you, Steve, it's probably better if you just don't even know who I'm really looking into."

Cain wouldn't tell him anyway, but he hoped the other man wouldn't ask. Cain respected Steve, had known him for a lot of years. He didn't want to let this drive a wedge—professional or personal—between them.

But he would if it meant catching the mole.

Steve rolled tense shoulders. "I don't like it, I'll be honest. But I like even less the thought of a traitor walking among us every day. Of more of my agents getting hurt or killed."

"I know," Cain said softly. "We're going to get

him, Steve. Get them. Freihof and whoever this mole is."

"Do you have any particular direction you're following?"

"Some. Based on profiling and what might be considered suspicious activities. Or even particular skill sets. But what's really going to help me catch this person is the computer stuff."

"That's why you're going to Hayley Green."

He could still see the way she'd looked at him that day in the courtroom. How dead her eyes had been. That had been the last time he'd seen her. He'd tried to visit her multiple times the first year she'd gone to prison, but she'd always refused to have anything to do with him. So then he'd stopped trying.

Although he'd never stopped thinking about her.

"I don't have the skills to find this person, but she does."

Steve's eyebrow raised. "You know Hayley is a convicted felon. You made sure of that."

His gut tightened at the thought, like it did every time. "But she's also the best at hacking a computer system."

"Are you sure she will help you?"

Hayley had been paroled four months ago. Cain knew the exact date she'd gotten out. He'd been surprised when she moved back to Gainesville, Georgia, upon release. The place she always said she wanted to get away from.

They both had wanted to get away from it. Heaven

knew they had spent enough time during their relationship in high school talking about getting out.
But maybe she had decided that familiar was better.

"Cain?" Steve repeated. "Are you sure that Hayley will help you? After everything that happened?"

Cain forced himself to release the tension in his
shoulders. "Hayley was guilty. She's now out of
prison and I'm sure she's ready to move on."

"But moving on and helping the man who put her
in prison are two different things."

Helping the man who used his relationship with
her to put her in prison.

Steve didn't say the words, but he didn't have to.
Both of them were thinking it; Steve had known Cain
when it happened. They both knew that was much
more difficult to move on from.

Cain ignored it. He'd done what he had to do four
years ago, even though it had gutted him. But the
law had been on his side. He tried to remember that.

And he'd had no idea the judge would be so hard
in his sentencing of Hayley. But that hadn't changed
the fact that she was guilty.

"Don't worry, I'll handle Hayley," Cain finally
said. And he would. He couldn't believe that she
wouldn't help him catch a murderer, no matter what
had transpired between the two of them in the past.

"If you say so." Steve wisely didn't say anything
further.

"I'm going to have to go completely dark from
Omega." Cain began stacking files. Many of them

would be coming with him to Georgia. "Hayley can't work anywhere within the Omega system."

"Completely dark?" Steve asked. "That could be dangerous. You won't have much backup if you need it."

"Until we know how deep this goes, have a better idea of who the mole is and what sort of capacity he or she has for obtaining information? I can't work within the Omega system. If this mole is as good as we think, he'll realize it if I'm inside."

The last thing either of them wanted to do was cause the traitor to go to ground. They'd never be able to catch him then. And that would make apprehending Freihof that much harder.

"The only people who will know what I'm doing will be you, Ren McClement in the DC office and me."

Steve nodded. They both wanted to trust more people but keeping this circle as small as possible was the best scenario. McClement worked in the highest levels of Omega Sector, bringing together multiple departments when needed. The man was all but a legend. Cain trusted Ren just as much as he trusted Steve.

With his life.

"You just be careful," Steve said. "Going dark can have some hard consequences."

"I'm willing to pay that price if it means we get this traitor out of our midst."

"I know you are." Steve studied him. "But sometimes we are not the only person to pay the price. Hayley might have been guilty of whatever crime she committed years ago, but dragging her into this could be even worse."

"Don't worry, I'll protect Hayley." Believe it or not, even if she couldn't see it, he'd always been trying to protect her. From the day he met her in high school until today. "I'll make sure it's cleared through the state so that she won't be violating her parole by helping us. I won't let anybody hurt her."

Steve moved toward the door, nodding. "I hope she sees it that way."

So did Cain.

Chapter Two

Hayley loaded the dirty dishes and wiped down the booth that had just been vacated by Bluewater Grill patrons. She slid along the soft gray leather of the seat to wipe a far corner of the table. She swiped at a few strands of dirty-blond hair that had escaped her long braid with the back of her hand, then hoped the moisture left on her forehead wasn't cleaning solution.

She almost moaned in relief at how good it felt to be off her feet for just a second as she wiped. It was two o'clock in the afternoon. She'd already been working six hours and still had another eight to go. Just like yesterday.

And the day before that.

It was the only way she could make ends meet when she earned only minimum wage. Less than that, actually. But she didn't argue, because at least she had a job.

Not many people were willing to hire a convicted felon, she'd found when she left the Georgia Women's

Correctional Institution four months ago. She'd been fortunate that the restaurant she worked at in high school part-time, still owned by the same family and now managed by their son, Timothy Smittle, a high school classmate of Hayley's, had been willing to take a chance on her.

They hadn't let her wait tables, explaining that they couldn't allow an ex-felon to interact with customers or handle money. But Timothy had graciously offered to allow Hayley to bus the tables, wash dishes and clean the entire restaurant.

The same Timothy who was looking over at her now, eyebrow raised, since she was no longer wiping the table, just resting. Hayley quickly jumped up, not wanting to risk another lecture about how lucky she was to have a job at such a respectable establishment.

Hayley didn't think too hard about her future. About the fact that she was twenty-eight years old, had no college degree, was an ex-felon and would probably still be working fourteen-hour days at the Bluewater twenty years from now.

Or the fact that she might have to start running for her life as soon as she was legally able to access a computer.

As she carried the bus pan back to the dishwashing area—thankful that some customer had come in and cut Timothy off from the route that had led straight to her and a lecture—she tried to count her blessings.

As a part of her parole she wasn't allowed to go

anywhere near a computer. The anklet she couldn't remove ensured she had no interaction with a computer that lasted longer than two minutes every six hours. Not even social media. Although maybe she could manage a tweet in under two minutes.

It was a prototype. She should probably feel honored that she was one of the first batch of cyber criminals it was being tested on. This was what happened when you were part of a high-profile crime that even grabbed the attention of US senators. Everybody wanted to make sure you didn't do it again.

Hayley had to admit her fingers itched for a keyboard. She yearned to get back into a world that involved no dishes or people like Smittle. She had a gift. When it came to computers and coding, she knew she had a gift.

Too bad she had let those gifts get her in trouble and cut her off from what could've been a very comfortable future. No one to blame but herself for that.

Well, maybe someone else to blame. But she didn't expect she would ever see Cain Bennett again, so there was no point in targeting any anger toward him.

She rubbed at an ache in the general vicinity of her heart at the thought of Cain. Then cursed herself not only for getting her shirt damp with her wet fingers, but for even thinking about him at all.

Plus, being away from computers was what was keeping her safe right now. As long as she couldn't go near a computer, she was not a threat to the people behind the situation that had led to her arrest and going to jail. Once they knew she could get near a computer and had the ability to trace their identities, Hayley had no doubt her life would become much more complicated.

But she couldn't touch a computer for another two years at least, so she would run screaming over that bridge when she got to it. She had more than enough trouble to deal with today.

Which led to her most important blessing. She could hear him entering the restaurant right now, even from the back.

"Mama Hay-lay!"

Hayley dried her hands on her apron and ripped it off, dropping it next to the dishwasher. She walked out into the front of the restaurant, strolling by Timothy without even pausing.

"I'm taking my hour break."

Timothy didn't argue. It was the one measure Hayley had demanded when she came to work here. That she would be given a break once a day, during the lull in the afternoon, when her cousin Ariel came by with little Mason.

Mason, Hayley's three-and-a-half-year-old son.

She grabbed Mason up in a hug, tickling him, breathing in his scent that meant so much to her, that calmed her and the tight spot inside her that grew whenever they were apart.

She and her son were together. They were both healthy, they were both happy, they were both free.

A piece of paper signed while Hayley was in prison had made Ariel Mason's legal guardian hours after his birth, but her cousin had made sure that Mason always knew Hayley was his mom.

Hayley wrapped her arm around Ariel also. "Hey, coz. Thanks again."

Hayley knew it had to be difficult for Ariel to get Mason here every day. They were trying to figure out exactly how to transition him back from Ariel's care to Hayley's with as little trauma as possible for Mason.

"No problem. It's the best part of our day."

Hayley's cousin had been a godsend. Hayley honestly had no idea what she would've done if it hadn't been for Ariel's willingness to care for Mason while Hayley was still incarcerated. He'd be a ward of the state otherwise.

Because there was no way in hell she would've told Cain he had a son. He'd made it very clear how little he thought of her when he'd used sex between them just to further his career by arresting her.

"It's raining outside, so do you want to go to the mall play area, champ?"

Little Mason nodded his head vigorously. "Yeah yeah yeah."

The drive to the mall took less than five minutes and soon they were watching Mason run around the enclosed area for children, made of soft foam material shaped like cars and rocket ships. It was one of Mason's favorite places to go.

Mason took after her—slender build, sandy-blond hair, and a zest for life that unfortunately had been driven out of her in prison. Hayley loved seeing the energy in Mason, and that energy fed her soul, especially on days when work seemed never ending.

"I know I sound like a broken record," Ariel said, taking a sip of the coffee she had picked up in the food court. "But you look exhausted."

Hayley rubbed her eyes and looked at the coffee with jealousy. She'd love to have the caffeine, but food court coffee was out of her budget. She didn't want to admit how good sitting down for an hour felt. "I'm okay, no need to worry."

"You're working twelve- to fourteen-hour days, six days a week. You can't tell me that's not taking a toll."

"It's not forever. I just want to make sure I'm as financially situated as possible before you leave."

Ariel took a sip of her coffee and worked to avoid making eye contact with Hayley. "About that… I've been thinking that maybe now isn't the right time. There will be another fellowship next year."

"No!" Hayley's tone brooked no refusal. "You've given up three years of your life for Mason and me. It's time for you to go do what you really want."

That included a full scholarship to Oxford, studying medieval literature for her master's degree. It was what Ariel had dreamed about her whole life. She'd postponed that dream to take in Mason, but Hayley refused to let her cousin give up any more time than she already had.

Ariel leaned over until her head touched the side of Hayley's shoulder. "I haven't given up zilch. If anything, I've gained. Mason has been a blessing."

Hayley leaned her cheek against the top of Ariel's head. "I'm sure you didn't think that during middle-of-the-night feedings when he was a newborn."

Hayley tamped down the heartbreak she still felt at having missed that part of her son's life. The important thing was that Mason had been cared for by someone who loved him.

"You're working yourself to the bone to try to make money for when I'm gone. If I applied for next year's fellowship you'd be in a much better situation."

Hayley wasn't just trying to save up money for Ariel's absence, but she didn't want to burden her cousin with any of that.

"But we both know they're not going to offer it to you again if you turn them down this year." They both watched as Mason ran up over a foam bridge. He'd already met another little boy and girl and was giggling with them both as they ran.

"There are other places I can study. Closer to home, not across the ocean."

"Ariel, you've done your part. I don't know how I would've survived without you. But you need to take care of yourself now. And Mason and I need to get to know each other, on our own. To become a mother and son."

Hayley had lived in the tiny apartment with Ariel and Mason since she'd gotten out of prison four months ago. Any hours she didn't spend working she spent with her son. And once Ariel left for Oxford, Hayley wouldn't be able to work these insane hours. Someone would need to be with Mason after day care, and Hayley planned to be that person.

So if she had to work herself nearly to death over the next two months to have enough money to get by while Ariel was gone, then she would damn well do that.

She would do whatever she had to in order to be able to live a normal life with her child.

"I know you don't like to talk about this, but what about contacting Mason's father?"

Hayley didn't even hesitate. "Not an option."

Ariel rolled her eyes. "You know I don't believe that nonsense about Mason's father being 'unknown' like you put on the birth certificate. There's no way you had some sort of one-night stand and didn't know the guy's name."

Hayley shrugged. "Yeah, well, we all make mistakes."

Cain Bennett had been hers.

All too soon it was time for Hayley to get back to the Bluewater. Ariel and Mason came inside to get Mason's normal scoop of Wednesday ice cream in the last few minutes Hayley had of her break.

Mason sat next to her in the booth and told about his friend he met at the play area.

"He came over and showed me his red car. Let me play with it," Mason said between bites.

Hayley reached over and kissed the top of his head. "Sounds like a pretty good friend you made there, buddy."

Mason moved on to talk about his favorite toys at preschool while Ariel and Hayley listened attentively.

Thank God Mason had taken to Hayley's presence in his life with such acceptance, that Ariel had constantly shown him pictures of Hayley and had referred to Hayley as his mom, had brought him for visitation in prison when she could. She and Ariel had done their best to make the transition natural and nondramatic. At first Hayley had just come over every day and gotten to know Mason. Two weeks later she moved in to the small apartment with them.

Hayley knew Mason loved her and that was all that mattered. When it came time for Ariel to go off to school it would be hard, but by then he would be even more comfortable with Hayley.

She saw Timothy looking over at her and then pointing at his watch. Hayley let out a sigh.

"Okeydoke guys, I've got to get back to work." Hayley stood up as Mason finished his last bite.

"I'm going to get this sugar-infested rug rat back home." Ariel smiled.

"I'll hopefully be getting off work at around seven thirty, so maybe I'll make it home in time for a bath and some book reading."

When Mason's face lit up at her words, Hayley

knew she would do whatever necessary to make it happen.

"I love it when you read me books! The fire truck book! The big banana book! The green ham and eggs book!" He bounced up and down on the seat, and she knew if she'd allowed him to stand on it, he'd be jumping with his excitement.

"All of them, little man, I promise. Okay?" Hayley laughed and reached down and scooped Mason up in her arms, hugging him probably a little too tightly.

"You squeezeded me!" Mason squealed, but hugged her back.

He'd always hugged her back. Hayley was oh so grateful that he'd never turned away from her, even at the beginning. She'd like to think it was because it was his child's heart responding to her mother's heart.

But it was probably just because he was a good kid and didn't want to hurt her feelings.

Hayley set Mason on the ground after giving him a loud kiss. "Get the books out and be ready. I'll see you tonight."

She watched as Mason took Ariel's hand and they walked out the door.

"That was an hour and six minutes, Hayley." Timothy had made his way over while she watched them leave.

Hayley turned back to the table to pick up the glasses and silverware. "Don't worry, Timothy, I will make sure I get all my work done."

"I agreed to this break every day, but now I'm thinking you're trying to take advantage of it."

Hayley managed to refrain from rolling her eyes. Barely. "It was six extra minutes. There's hardly anybody in the restaurant and I have plenty of time to get everything done before the dinner rush starts."

"Well, I just don't want six extra minutes to turn into ten extra minutes to turn into thirty extra minutes. After all, we did do you a big favor by hiring you here."

Hayley didn't argue, just continued to clear off the table. Timothy Smittle was getting her labor at less cost than he would have to pay others. She was doing the work of two people and barely getting paid one person's salary.

But she didn't have any other choice, so she would keep her opinions and her arguments to herself. This was temporary. Mason was forever. Whatever she had to do to reestablish herself, to be prepared to take care of him in any situation, she would do it.

"Someone is coming in the door right now. All the waitresses are on break, so I'll seat him and you take his order. But don't do anything having to do with money. I'll give him his check after."

And keep the tip for himself, no doubt.

Hayley let out a weary sigh. "Fine, Timothy. Just let me go get my apron on and I'll take his order."

Hayley refused to let the exhaustion overwhelm her, even though she felt it much more now that

Mason was gone. She would work hard, get through the shift and get home to her baby.

She grabbed a glass of water for the table where she needed to take the order. She was almost there, pulling her friendly facade over her features, when she looked up at the restaurant guest.

The water slipped out of her numb fingers and shattered as it hit the hardwood floor.

Cain Bennett.

Her eyes ran over his face. Not much had changed in the four years since she'd last seen him. His forceful chin and chiseled jaw were still completed by broad cheekbones, five-o'clock shadow already clear on them even at this early hour. His dark hair was still cut short, but with that rebellious curl that tended to fall across his forehead.

Those same green eyes with flecks of brown were now full of concern as he stood, staring at her. Cain hadn't just happened to walk into this restaurant. He was here specifically looking for her.

Under no circumstance could this possibly be good.

Chapter Three

Cain approached Hayley slowly, both arms outstretched. Not unlike how he had approached traumatized victims in the past.

Because that's exactly how Hayley looked: traumatized. Hell, she hadn't looked this drained even in court four years ago.

Now her brown eyes had shadows under them, outlining an obvious exhaustion. She looked like she could gain another ten pounds and still be a little underweight.

And she was staring at him with something akin to terror in her eyes.

Cain hadn't expected her to be happy to see him, but neither had he expected her to look like she was carrying the world's weight on her shoulders. A sort of panic itched at his gut.

He took a step closer. She took a step back.

"Hayley, what the heck happened?" The manager rushed out from the back. "Get something to clean that up."

The man turned and faced Cain. "We're so sorry about this. I'll get you another— Cain? Cain Bennett?"

Cain dragged his eyes away from Hayley to look at the man who knew his name. "Yes?"

"It's Timothy Smittle. We went to high school together, remember, man?"

"I'll go get a mop," Hayley murmured before turning and almost running into the kitchen.

Timothy hooked a thumb toward Hayley's retreating form. "And of course, you remember Hayley Green, right? You guys were all hot and heavy back in the day."

"Of course." Cain slowly sat back down in the booth, eyes fixed on the door Hayley had exited through.

Timothy slid into the booth across from Cain and lowered his voice even though there was no one else around. "And I guess you heard about the law trouble Hayley got into a few years back. That was after you had already left. She did some time at the Georgia Women's Correctional."

Cain just nodded.

"When she came back around here begging for her old job, I figured it was the least we could do. You know, since we all went to high school together." Timothy sounded very pleased with himself. Like he was collecting bonus points or something.

Cain's eyes left the door and moved to Timothy.

"She helped you with your bookkeeping in high school, right? Is that what she's doing now?"

Timothy smirked. "Are you kidding? We couldn't let her near anything having to do with money."

Cain's lips pressed together although he knew he really couldn't blame Timothy. "So she's what, waiting tables?"

The thought of someone with Hayley's intelligence and skills waiting tables was difficult for Cain to swallow, but he guessed he shouldn't be surprised. Right now her job options were probably limited.

Timothy shifted a little uncomfortably in the booth across from Cain. "Um, well, that also involves money, so no. Mostly she's, you know, helping out doing other things."

Before Cain could press about exactly what those "other things" were, Hayley came back out with a broom and mop and began cleaning up the glass and water she'd spilled.

"I can help." Cain slid to the edge of the booth ready to stand.

Timothy laughed out loud. "No, Cain. You sit down. It's Hayley's job."

Hayley didn't look up from what she was doing, but Cain could see the flush spread across her cheeks. She quickly swept up the glass and mopped up the water.

"So, how have you been, man?" Timothy asked, as if they'd been best buddies in high school. Cain barely recalled talking to the other guy at all. "You went on to play ball in college, right? After leading us to the state championships?"

"Yeah, for a couple of years. Then I blew out my knee. Nothing to stop normal life, but effectively ended my football career."

Hayley had finished cleaning up and Cain could tell she was hesitating about whether to stay nearby or to leave. Timothy noticed it, too.

Timothy waved a dismissive hand in Hayley's direction. "You can go do your work in the back. I'll take Cain's order and get him what he needs."

Hayley still wasn't looking at Cain, but he didn't want her to leave. "Actually, I'm here to talk to Hayley."

Timothy stiffened. "Oh. Actually, Hayley just took a break with Ariel and the kid, so she doesn't have another break for a few hours."

Cain looked around, noticing that Hayley became even more tense with Timothy's words. It was three o'clock in the afternoon and the place was nearly empty.

"It doesn't look like you really need her right at this second. I just need to borrow her for a few minutes."

Timothy turned to glare at Hayley as if she had planned this. "Actually, during the downtime is when Hayley does most of the dishes and cleaning in the back. Then she helps out in front during the rushes."

Hayley was the damned *dishwasher*?

"It's fine, Timothy. I'm not going to take another

break. I don't have anything to say to Cain anyway." She still wouldn't look at him.

Cain had figured it would come down to this. Taking out his Omega Sector credentials, he turned back to Timothy. "This is law enforcement business. Hayley isn't in any trouble and isn't wanted by the law, but I need to talk to her about a few things. I'd appreciate it if we could have your cooperation."

He saw Hayley stiffen further out of the corner of his eye.

Timothy stood. "Well, I don't want to get in the way of the law, but really we don't pay Hayley to sit around and talk to old boyfriends. I'll go get you your water."

Timothy left, shaking his head. Hayley finally looked at Cain. "Yeah, this isn't a good time. I'm working."

She seemed genuinely nervous about being here talking to him. Maybe she was afraid she was going to lose her job. Such as it was. "I can come to your house later if you want." He had her address from her parole file.

"No," she immediately said. "I don't want you coming there."

"Okay." He held his hands out in a gesture of peace. "If you don't want to talk here and you don't want to talk at your home, maybe we can meet for dinner tonight?"

She shook her head again. "I can't. I'm working here until seven thirty and then I have to go straight home."

Cain refused to let himself get annoyed at her avoidance. "How about early tomorrow, then? What time does your shift start?"

"Seven a.m." She shrugged.

He felt himself stiffen. "Did you begin working today at seven a.m. also?"

She shrugged. "I'm working a lot of hours this week."

By the look of her exhausted face and the weight she'd lost, it had been more than just this week that she'd been working a lot of hours.

"What are you doing here, Hayley? Why are you working *here*?"

Her eyes narrowed at him. "Believe it or not, there's not a lot of options out there for an ex-felon with no college degree. Especially since a condition of my parole is that I'm not allowed near a computer for more than two minutes at a time."

She stuck out her ankle and pulled her khaki pants up just a little bit. Cain could see the electronic monitor strapped around her slim leg.

"It's a prototype. Lets everybody know if I'm a naughty girl. So when Timothy was nice enough to give me a job—albeit, washing dishes and cleaning the kitchen—I took it."

Even after she'd refused to see him while in prison, he'd tried to keep tabs on her from a distance. Life in a minimum security facility wasn't terribly difficult, not like a medium or maximum security facility, but it still wasn't freedom.

He had to admit he hadn't really thought about what her life would be like once she actually was released. That the agreement of her parole might stop her from using her natural abilities and skills.

And so here she was with her genius IQ and incredible computer aptitude, washing dishes and mopping floors.

Guilt started to eat at him, but Cain squashed it down. Hayley had broken the law. Cain had been doing his job when he arrested her. But allowing them to get physically involved while he was on the case had been the biggest mistake of his professional life. Something he would always regret. The one thing he couldn't blame Hayley for hating him for.

Hayley was still standing there when Timothy brought the glass of water back out. "Do you want to order anything?"

Cain turned to Timothy. "No, I'm just going to steal about five minutes of Hayley's time. I really appreciate it, Timothy. For old times and all." He smiled at the other man.

Feeling important again, Timothy grinned back. "It's no problem. Anything for Gainesville's greatest high school football star."

"That was a lot of years ago, man. And I was far from the greatest."

"Not to those of us who stuck around here." Timothy turned to Hayley. "We'll just count your break as an hour and a half today, cool?"

Hayley's lips tightened, but she nodded. Timothy walked off again.

"What do you want, Cain? Why are you here? How long have you been here?"

"Been here in town?"

"No, here at the restaurant."

"I just walked in a second ago. Why?"

Hayley studied him for a minute, looking relieved. "Never mind, it doesn't matter. But what do you want?"

"Why don't you sit down? You look like you could use a few minutes' break."

Hayley's eyebrows arched but she did what he asked.

"Do you need something to eat?" he asked. She looked like she hadn't had a solid meal in months. "I could order something for us both."

She ignored his question. "Why are you here, Cain? I know it's not to have a meal. I know you're not stupid enough to come back here for a social visit."

Cain could feel a muscle tightening in his jaw. "No, I'm here on business."

He could see her visibly tense. "I haven't done anything that violates my parole. Haven't broken any laws."

Of course that was why she would think he was here. Why wouldn't she? "No. When I said I was here on business I didn't mean to arrest you or anything like that. You're not in any trouble."

She still didn't relax. "Fine. Then what did you need to talk to me about? I need to get back to work, Cain. Some of us get paid by the hour."

"And how many hours a week do you have to work here to make ends meet? You look tired." He touched her hand lying on the table before he could think better of it.

She snatched it away as if she'd been burned.

"No." Her voice was hoarse. "You don't get to be concerned about me. Ever. You gave up that right four years ago."

"When I had you arrested? You were guilty, Hayley. Guilty of using your computer skills for hacking."

She laughed, but the sound held no amusement whatsoever. "You know what? I've had a long time to think about this. To categorize and figure out exactly how I felt about everything that happened with my arrest and incarceration. You were a federal agent, I was a criminal. It was your job to catch me—I've never blamed you for that."

She slid to the edge of the booth. "When those cops barged into my apartment to arrest me, I wasn't surprised. I think I'd always known I would eventually get caught."

Cain wanted to feel relief that she didn't blame him. That she understood he'd been doing his job. But he knew there was more.

She stared at him. He almost wished it was with

fury rather than the exhaustion that seemed to blanket both her body and spirit. "Then I saw *you*. Realized you were the one in charge of the investigation. Realized you had deliberately used the feelings we had for each other, the connection we'd always had, to get close to me."

He started to interrupt, but she held out a hand to stop whatever he might say.

"You seduced me in order to arrest me, Cain. And it nearly cost me everything." Hayley stood. "So whatever business it is you want to talk to me about? Forget it. We have nothing to say to each other."

Chapter Four

The next morning before the sun was even up, Cain sat in the diner a few blocks away from the Bluewater Grill. Hayley was supposed to meet him here in twenty minutes.

She damn well better show up. When she'd walked away yesterday, he'd let her go. But he'd stayed, had lunch, even suffered through an hour of reminiscing with Timothy.

When Hayley had come out of the kitchen to refill the ice in the server's station, he'd caught her glance. He'd seen her big brown eyes widen, then narrow, from all the way across the restaurant.

Eventually she'd made her way back over to him.

"Why are you still here?"

He'd leaned back in the booth like he didn't have anywhere else in the world to be. "Because you haven't listened to what I have to say yet."

For just a second she'd looked at him as though she would like to push him into oncoming traffic. Cain didn't mind. He would take that any day over how breakable she'd looked a couple of hours before. "Fine. If I listen to you, will you leave?"

"It will take more than two sentences. You'll have to sit down. Give me a few minutes."

Hayley had looked over her shoulder at Timothy, who'd been glaring. And just like that the anger was gone. Breakable was back.

"I can't." She started loading dishes off his table and putting them in the bin she'd carried out. "I don't have any more time today."

Damn it. Cain had wanted to punch something. And it might have been Timothy if he'd started harassing Hayley again. But that would've just added to her distress.

"You're working a double tomorrow, too?" he asked.

She'd nodded and wiped down his table.

"Fine. Meet me for breakfast at the diner down the block in the morning before your shift starts."

She grimaced. "Fine. Six thirty. You'll have thirty minutes."

He'd left after that. Mostly because he couldn't bear to stay in there and watch Hayley work so hard and look so damn fragile.

Forget the mole, all he wanted to do was steal Hayley away from here, take her to a beach house somewhere and let her just sit out in the sun.

And feed her, for God's sake. Meal after meal until she finally put enough weight on to be considered *thin*. And exhaustion and fear didn't blanket her every expression.

Cain scrubbed a hand over his face. He felt like he was missing some important piece of this puzzle. He could understand why Hayley was working at the Bluewater, and even the difficulty in getting a job. But why the hell was she working herself to the bone? The cost of living in Georgia wasn't so high that she needed to work eighty hours a week to get by.

What the hell had happened to her? Had life in prison been that bad? Or adjusting back into society that difficult? Hayley was so damn smart. He'd halfway thought she would use her time incarcerated to plan a new business or get her college degree. Maybe the no-computers decree had disrupted whatever plans she'd made.

She obviously needed money in a pretty desperate way. Omega was willing to pay her a hefty consultant's fee for her help in catching the mole.

Of course, Cain was also going to have to carefully watch where that money was being spent. There weren't a lot of good reasons he could think of that would have her working herself into the ground, but there were a lot of bad ones.

Buying her way back into the den of hackers was the most obvious. Maybe she had to have a certain dollar amount by the time her computer restrictions were lifted on her parole.

Cain's hands clenched into fists. He'd be damned if he was going to let her drop back into that life again.

So maybe this mission was going to serve more

than one purpose: catch the mole inside Omega and save Hayley from herself.

But first she had to show up this morning. Even if it was only so Cain could feed her.

He got a cup of coffee and put in an order for a full breakfast for both of them about ten minutes before Hayley was scheduled to arrive. He wasn't going to let not having enough time be an excuse not to eat. Although he was hoping to talk her out of going to work altogether. The consultant's fee would be at least five times what she would make busing tables and washing dishes.

He saw her instantly as she entered the diner, long blond hair pulled back in a braid. She had a large canvas bag over one shoulder and was already in her Bluewater T-shirt and khaki pants. Damn restaurant didn't even open for another four hours, so why the hell did she need to go in so early?

He knew the moment she saw him, tension shooting into her small frame like someone had fused a metal pipe to her spine. He stood as she got to their booth. She at least looked a little less tired than yesterday afternoon.

"I don't have long. I have to clock in by seven," she said by way of greeting.

"Good morning." He ignored her abrupt words as she slid into the booth across from him.

"This isn't a date, Cain. Not even a breakfast between friends. Tell me what it is you have to say."

He slid into the seat across from her. "We'll talk with breakfast."

"I don't have time for breakfast."

"Tough. I already ordered for both of us."

She glared at him, fire burning even higher in her eyes when the waitress brought their food less than a minute later.

"Presumptuous much?"

He just shrugged. "Everybody's got to eat. You more than most."

"What are you trying to say, Bennett?"

He definitely didn't want to get into a fight with her and cause her to not eat just out of spite. "I'm saying you're working a double today. So you need to eat."

He dug in to his own food, relieved a few moments later when she did the same.

"You got what I liked. Thank you," she said softly.

Fried eggs, hash browns with all the fixings, sausage, bacon. Nothing sweet. She'd always said sweet food made her coffee—which she took with a god-awful amount of cream and sugar—not taste sweet enough. He'd never forgotten, didn't think he ever would.

He nodded and kept eating, waiting until she had a huge bite of food in her mouth before asking his next questions.

"Why are you working so hard, Hayley? At the Bluewater. Why so many double shifts?"

She looked like she was going to light into him.

He expected it, actually, thus the timing of his question when she couldn't easily answer.

"I know it's partially because finding a job as an ex-felon isn't easy and you took what you could get. But you shouldn't have to be working so hard that you're exhausted all the time. Timothy mentioned you work as many hours as you can every week."

The man had also said it as though he'd been doing Hayley some great favor by allowing her to work that much.

She shrugged, finally finished chewing. "That's what you have to do when you're not even making minimum wage."

Cain's eyes narrowed. "Unless you're waiting tables or something where you're making tips, he's required by law to pay you at least minimum wage."

"You stay out of it. I will handle Timothy." That pinched look was back in her eyes. Cain wasn't trying to add to her stress.

"Even if he isn't paying you quite minimum wage—" and Cain would be looking into that "—you still shouldn't need to work eighty hours a week to get by here in Gainesville. It's not like Georgia has some ridiculously high cost of living."

"Is that what you brought me here for? To remind me that I have a crappy job and pretty crappy future ahead of me?"

"Hayley—"

"I already made my feelings about the arrest clear yesterday. As for every other part of my life, including when or how long I work, it's none of your business."

He held out a hand in surrender. He didn't want this to get out of control. "Okay, fine. Just finish eating, okay?" If he had his way she would eat everything on that plate and then another whole one after that.

She took another bite and he relaxed a little. But he was running out of time.

And what did he expect, that she was just going to tell him everything going on in her life? Especially if it had to do with potentially illegal activities.

"I brought you here to offer you a job. With Omega Sector."

Her eyes narrowed in suspicion. "What kind of job could you possibly want me for?"

"We need your computer skills to catch someone providing critical information to a specific criminal."

"Doesn't Omega Sector have its own computer crimes division?"

Cain nodded. "Yes. But we have a mole inside Omega. A good one. I need someone who's even better, who's not in law enforcement. That's you."

"I'm not the only great hacker."

"You're the only one I know I can trust."

She rolled her eyes. "I can't believe you can even say that with a straight face."

He set his coffee cup back down. "When it comes to this, I do trust you. Completely. You may have made some questionable decisions four years ago, for whatever reason, but I know you wouldn't want to ever hurt anyone. The person we're trying to find is a murderer, Hayley."

He thought of Grace Parker's face as Freihof's knife slit her throat. Catching the mole inside Omega would be a direct link to putting him away for good.

"Yeah, I'm not a murderer at least."

"Of course you're not. I hope you know I never thought you would hurt somebody else. No matter what damage you might be able to do with a computer, you've always had too big a heart to hurt people."

She stirred the last of her hash browns around on her plate.

"Look, Cain." It was the most gentle tone he'd heard from her. "I don't really have time for another job. The Bluewater keeps me pretty busy. Plus, I'm not allowed near computers as part of my parole agreement."

"Actually, I'm hoping you'll be able to find the mole's movements by looking through files of code I've printed. Won't need you near a computer."

He took out the file that held the contract for the work Omega wanted her to do, including what she would be paid, and slid it over so she could see it. He felt better when her eyes got a little wide at the number. Although, damn it, that meant the Bluewater really was paying her below minimum wage.

"This amount is to complete the project. Find the traitor inside Omega. That might take you a day, might take you three weeks. If it takes longer than either of us are thinking, then we'll renegotiate for a larger amount."

Cain knew she'd already read the contract, at least the pertinent details. Hayley could read twice as fast as the average person. But she still wasn't looking up at him, giving him any indication if she was going to say yes.

"Hays." He used his old high school nickname for her and reached out and touched her hand where it sat on the table. "I will help you. Whatever is going on, whatever reason you're working yourself to death, even if you're inching yourself back toward trouble, I'll help you. You help me catch this mole, and I'll help you with whatever it is that's weighing so heavily on you."

HAYLEY LOOKED AT where Cain's big hand rested over hers, so strong and capable.

His words, the promise behind them, were just like old times. Back when it was the two of them against the world.

God, she was so tired. She wanted to lean into his strength. She wanted to tell him about everything— about Mason, about the people she was afraid would be coming after them once she could go near a computer again, about *everything*.

But that would be the worst possible thing she could do. Might cost her all she held precious. She couldn't lose Mason again. And if Cain found out he had a son and decided he wanted custody, what judge wouldn't give it to him over a mother who was an ex-con with dubious future employment?

She slid her hand out from under his, the touch too painful a reminder of what was never going to be again. She really didn't blame Cain for the arrest, but they were never going to go back to what they were.

She picked up the contract, glancing at it again. The money. This might really make a difference for her. For getting out of the hole, being ready to run with Mason if needed.

She couldn't turn down this amount of money, even if it would be dangerous working with Cain.

"Okay, I'll do it."

She could see relief all across his handsome features. That black curl sliding toward his forehead as it always had. He looked so comfortable sitting there in his black T-shirt and jeans. She forced herself to look away. It wasn't fair that she could still be attracted to him after all these years and after everything that had happened between them.

"You'll have to quit your job at the Bluewater," he said.

"I'm going to need that job after this project for Omega Sector is finished. It's not great but at least it's regular, dependable work."

He looked like he was going to argue. But finally just said, "Fine, but you'll have to take a leave of absence for a few weeks."

Hayley nodded although she had no plan to do that. First of all, Timothy would never go for a "leave of absence." He'd just fire her. Second, since she was going through papers, she could do that when she wasn't working. Maybe she might have to cut back on a couple of shifts, but it would be worth it.

"Can you start today? Time is of the essence in catching this guy."

"Guy?" Hayley raised an eyebrow. "You're assuming your mole is male?"

"Actually, one of my prime suspects is female. I definitely have no assumptions of gender when it comes to crime."

Was that an insult against Hayley personally? Or was it just that Cain was too good at his job to be fooled by someone just because of their gender? And Cain was an excellent agent, she had no doubt about that.

"I'll have to go in to the restaurant for at least a couple hours. I can't just leave them in a lurch. But then I'll clear off as much of my schedule as I can."

Cain nodded. "I thought we could work out of my parents' house. They moved down to Florida, but still kept the place here."

Hayley's lips tightened. She didn't necessarily want to go back to the place where they spent so much time in high school. But what choice did she have? She definitely didn't want Cain coming to her apartment and seeing Mason.

"Fine. I'll meet you there in a few hours. You know this would go much more quickly if I could scroll through a computer screen rather than have to read code on paper, right?"

Suspicion immediately shuttered his features. "Paper. That's what we're working with. No computers." His tone was final.

He thought she was going to get back into trouble if she could get online. If only he knew trouble was going to find her as soon as she did. Possibly the worst kind of trouble.

She'd worry about that another day. Right now she had to worry about how she was going to work day in and day out with one of the best agents of the most prestigious law enforcement agency in the country while keeping the biggest possible secret from him.

Chapter Five

The strands of printed code began to blur in front of her eyes and Hayley's head jerked up as it started to fall forward in sleep.

"Whoa there, girl, you all right?" asked Mara, the Bluewater's newest employee, setting a cup of coffee on the desk near the papers Hayley was going through.

The beautiful smell of it revived Hayley slightly, at least enough to pry her eyes open. "Coffee. You're a goddess, Mara. Thank you so much."

"Honey, I know we don't know each other very well, but you are looking at those papers all the dang time." Mara's thick Southern accent coated the words. "Every time you're on a break, before a shift, after a shift. Heck, I wouldn't be surprised to see you carrying in a ream of papers when you go on a bathroom break."

For four days Hayley had been scouring the computer code printouts Cain had given her. The first day she'd met Cain over at his parents' old house and, studiously forgetting that the bed in which they'd first made love was just right upstairs, they'd pored over the files together.

That afternoon he'd received a call and had to leave to go to one of the Omega Sector offices. So he'd given Hayley the printouts of the computer code, all six huge legal file boxes of them, to work on while he was gone for two or three days.

He'd expected her to be working on them every day. And she had. She'd brought them home that night and studied them deep into the night after spending time with Mason and putting him to bed.

She'd brought a box to the Bluewater with her and, like Mara pointed out, had been going over them every spare second she had. Unfortunately that hadn't been much since she'd worked three double shifts in a row, fourteen hours a day each.

She talked to Timothy about reducing her hours, but when he'd started murmuring about hiring someone to take her place, Hayley knew she couldn't do it. His hiring Mara had scared her enough and she was mostly just a waitress. She was not going to take Hayley's job.

She needed to make more progress on the computer code, but she couldn't afford to lose the livelihood she would need once Cain was gone. Of course, if she didn't find some answers soon, Cain might fire her and try to find someone else to help.

"Honey, what is that stuff?" Mara asked as Hayley

took a sip of her coffee. "I glanced at it but it didn't seem to make a bit of sense to me."

Hayley smiled at the older woman with big brassy blond hair. "Computer code."

"What are you reading computer code for? Do you do that for fun?" Mara's look placed the thought just above root canals.

"I do like computers, I have to admit. But no, this is not what I do for fun. This is actually sort of a job."

"For Timothy? Is it something to do with the restaurant?"

Hayley stood up, stretching her back. "Speaking of, I've got to get back out on the floor. Tim will be looking for me I'm sure." It was her fifteen-minute evening break, but like every break she used it to look back over the coding.

"He won't mind if you're late if you're doing something for him."

Hayley shook her head. "No, this is not for him. This is sort of a side job for me."

"Oh." Mara's eyes got big. "I didn't know you did side jobs with computer codes."

Hayley ran a hand over her tired eyes. "Only when my past comes back to haunt me."

She didn't wait to hear what Mara would say about that cryptic statement, just headed to the back of the kitchen where she could begin washing dishes. She left the box of papers there in the supply closet. Hardly anyone went in and even if they did, unless they were well versed in computer coding, none of the pages would make sense.

Weariness set heavily on her shoulders, her muscles sore, her brain tired. She needed more than the four hours of sleep she was getting each night. Needed a chance to do something else besides work here or filter through the code.

She hadn't even seen Mason in two days. She told herself it was okay as she loaded a rack of dishes into the dishwasher. She knew she had to take this opportunity while it was here to make such great money.

But she lived in constant fear that her son would forget her. That no matter how often Ariel talked to him about Hayley, he would reject her somewhere inside.

Guilt battled with exhaustion, and for the first time she was glad for all the steam that flew out of the industrial dishwasher. At least it hid her tears.

Three hours later, nearly ready to drop, Hayley had all her work finished in the kitchen. Mara and the other waitresses had left. Timothy was on his way to make the night bank deposit and had closed up the entire front of the restaurant. All Hayley needed to do was mop the floors and she could go.

The thought of dragging the mop over the entire restaurant was completely beyond her at this moment. She'd have another cup of coffee, look over a little more of the code and then mop.

And then go home for four or five hours of sleep. And then get back up and do the same thing again tomorrow.

The only light at the end of the tunnel was that for the first time today she'd seen an odd pattern in the coding. It might be nothing, but the way the data had been sent in that particular transmission had been odd, as if it possibly housed some other message.

It wasn't much but it was at least something to look for, to see if it happened again. Once she had a pattern it would be easier to find how the mole was communicating.

Of course all of this would be a hell of a lot easier if she could look at it on the screen, scrolling down as she finished each section, rather than having to physically get a new sheet of paper to look at. But she wouldn't complain. She was making money.

Cain was going to be back soon—was supposed to have been back yesterday—and was probably going to blow a gasket when he found out she was *still* working at the Bluewater, rather than just for him full-time. She would just have to make him understand that she needed this job, too.

She made her coffee, dragging out the cream and sugar—hoping Timothy wouldn't decide this was employee theft—and made her way back to the tiny desk inside the not-much-bigger supply closet.

The coffee provided mental fortitude enough for her to confirm the first suspicious pattern she'd seen in the coding earlier today and look for it again. All she needed was to see the same loophole the mole had attempted twice and she would have what she needed.

But after another hour, pages highlighted and spread all over the stockroom, her lids were heavy again. She'd done all she could do for today. She needed to mop and go home.

The sound of the front glass breaking had Hayley bolting upright, all exhaustion gone. She jerked open the closet door and found the hallway engulfed in flames.

The building was on fire? How had it spread into the hallway so soon and why was it growing so fast?

More importantly, how the hell was she going to get out of here when the entire hall was engulfed in flames?

Going back into the supply closet, already starting to cough, she grabbed her cell and called 911. In the few moments it took for her to get connected to an operator, more smoke was seeping under the door.

"911. State your emergency."

"I'm at the Bluewater Grill." Hayley coughed out the address. "There's a fire. I'm trapped inside."

As she said the words, panic barreled through her. Oh God, she really was trapped inside. She wasn't going to be able to get past the fire in the hall.

The operator was telling her to stay low, that help was coming. Hayley could barely hear the woman's words over her own panicked breaths and coughs.

There was no way she would survive until the

fire department got here. She needed to get out of this room before the fire made it all the way in. The chemicals surrounding her would be lethal if she breathed them in, and might even explode.

She grabbed her T-shirt and yanked it over her mouth and nose before opening the door. Heat blasted her back, stealing her breath. Through narrowed eyes she saw that the flames had now encompassed the entire hall—walls, floor and ceiling. She would have to run through the hall—maybe seven or eight feet, all a blazing inferno.

"Hayley!"

Someone was calling her from the other end of the hallway.

Cain.

"Cain!" She yelled as loud as she could, but the word came out as a croak.

He would never hear her voice. Would have no idea she was back here. She rushed back into the supply room and grabbed a wrench and metal can of paint. *Please let it be enough.*

She brought it back in the hallway and began banging on it with every bit of failing strength she had left.

"Hayley, is that you?"

She banged harder.

"Hang on, I'll be right back," he yelled.

She dropped the can and wrench, falling back from the flames that were crawling closer to her. A few moments later he was back. She heard a fire extinguisher being sprayed in spurts and then could see him in the flames coming toward her. Big, strong, capable.

He yanked her into his arms. "Are you okay?"

She nodded.

"Stay close to me. We've got to move fast. Keep low."

He pulled her in front of him, wrapping his body protectively around hers, using the extinguisher he held in front of her, making a path for them. Hayley felt heat all around her as they moved, but nothing burned. Cain's arm kept her waist tucked against him, his back sheltering her from the fire that flamed behind them once they moved past.

Out of the hallway the immediate danger subsided, but the entire dining room of the restaurant was on fire. Cain pulled her through and out the front door, both desperately sucking in oxygen as they hit clean air.

"Are you okay?" he asked again once they could breathe, sitting at the far end of the parking lot, watching the fire trucks roll in.

"Yes." Her voice sounded rusty. Hoarse. But already her lungs were easing.

He yanked her into his arms again, cradling her head against his chest. She let out a little squeak but didn't try to get away. That had been way too close. Things had gone from fine to critical so quickly she wasn't even sure exactly what had happened.

And definitely didn't know what would've happened if Cain hadn't shown up when he did. She tried to ease her head back from his grasp, but he wouldn't let her.

"Why were you at the Bluewater?" she croaked out.

"I went by your apartment."

Now Hayley completely jerked away from him. Had he seen Mason? Oh God, what was she supposed to say?

"I talked to your cousin. Who, of course, wouldn't even let me in the door."

Relief flooded her. Ariel didn't know Cain was Mason's father, and even if she suspected it was him, Ariel wouldn't say anything to him. She was still mad about the whole arrest thing.

"And," he continued, glaring down at her, "imagine my surprise when Ariel told me you were at work. Here at the Bluewater. From where, if I recall, we agreed you would get time off."

"I tried, but it didn't work out and I couldn't afford to get fired. Don't worry, I've still been doing your work. I just—"

Cain's livid curse cut her off. "I don't care about the damn case, Hayley. You were already bone-weary exhausted before I got here. And now you added searching the computer codes in your *spare time*?"

Hayley looked over at the restaurant, which was now completely up in flames. All the files she had gone through over the last four days, any progress she had made, were now gone.

Maybe she would tell him that after he had calmed down about the fact that she had two jobs. Because right now she didn't have the energy to fight, or really to do anything but sit here and breathe.

But it wasn't long before the fire department had the burning building under control and everyone had questions. Cain stayed by her side, features pinched, as Hayley explained that she'd been in the back room reading. Cain confirmed that she was doing some consulting work for Omega Sector.

When the fire inspector explained that the entire back half of the restaurant had been completely destroyed, Hayley looked over at Cain.

"All my work with the computer codes is gone. It was all here with me."

"You shouldn't have even been here in the first place," he muttered. "But printouts are replaceable."

At least he didn't seem too mad about how this was going to set them back. He was much angrier about her being here at the restaurant.

Timothy joined them not long after and Hayley was definitely glad to have Cain around to calm the other man down. Timothy wanted to know exactly what had happened and Hayley had no idea.

"You must've left something on in the kitchen," Timothy screamed. "This is all your fault."

"Actually," the fire inspector cut in, "we have pretty irrefutable proof that this fire was arson related."

"Arson?" Timothy scoffed. "That's ridiculous.

You're saying someone burned the restaurant on purpose?"

Timothy turned and glared at Hayley again. "Maybe some of your old prison buddies or something?"

Hayley didn't even know how to respond to that. But she didn't have to. She felt Cain's hand slide around her waist and pull her back slightly so that he could step in front of her, putting himself between her and Timothy.

Cain turned to the fire inspector. "You said you had proof?"

"Looks like three good old-fashioned Molotov cocktails. Thrown straight through the windows."

"What the hell is a Molotov cocktail?" Timothy spit out.

"Poor man's grenade," Cain muttered.

The fire inspector nodded. "Yep. They're also called bottle bombs. Basically a can of some sort of flammable liquid, with a burning wick sticking out. It gets thrown and sets everything it touches on fire."

"And if it came through the front window, then Hayley was very definitely not involved," Cain pointed out to Timothy.

"Actually, how the fire in that back hallway escalated so quickly is something we'll be checking into. So I'd appreciate it if everyone wouldn't mind staying in touch."

"I'm sure she had something to do with it." Timothy turned to point at Hayley. "She just got out of prison."

"Timmy, I know you and I went to school together, but we're going to have a problem if you keep this up," Cain said, tone hard.

The fire inspector turned to Timothy. "In my years of experience, I've found that the people who almost died in the fire are not responsible for the arson. I've also found that in many arson cases involving a business, the owner has something to do with it."

Hayley somehow managed not to laugh at Timothy's outraged look.

"Oh my gosh, Hayley honey, are you okay?" Hayley heard Mara's Southern drawl as the woman rushed up behind her. "I just heard about the fire on the news and I rushed back over here. I knew you had been the last person here."

Cain continued to talk to the fire inspector and Timothy as Hayley turned to talk to Mara.

"Yeah, it was pretty scary." Hayley really didn't want to think about how seriously close to death she'd come tonight. "If my friend Cain hadn't come by, I would've been trapped."

Mara threw her arms around Hayley. "I'm so glad you're okay. Did you lose all your stuff you've been working on so hard? All your computer papers?"

Hayley nodded. "It was all I could do to get out with my life."

Evidently the older woman was a hugger, as she threw her arms around Hayley again. "The important thing is, you're all right."

Hayley could feel exhaustion pulling at her. She

needed to get home. Although it looked like nobody would have to work at the Bluewater tomorrow.

"Looks like none of us will be working here for a while," Hayley said. "We'll all have to find new jobs."

Given the fact that Timothy thought she had something to do with it, Hayley doubted she would be working there ever again.

"Yeah, that's a bummer," Mara said. "But I hope you and I can keep in touch even with new jobs."

Hayley nodded. She didn't have friends. Surviving and providing had taken up all her time since she'd gotten out of prison. "I'd like that."

Mara hugged Hayley once more and then moved on. Hayley saw Cain still talking to the fire inspector and made her way back to him.

"I'm going home. I'm tired," she whispered.

Tired didn't even come close to what she was feeling. At this point Hayley was afraid she wasn't going to be able to even walk over to her car, much less drive home.

But, like always, she would find a way.

She turned, but Cain grabbed her elbow. "No."

"Whatever needs to be talked about is going to have to wait." Everything around her was starting to spin slightly. Crap. She needed to get to her car so she could at least sit down.

"I'll drive you," Cain said. "But we're not going to your house. I'll take you back to my place."

"No." She wanted to make a more elaborate argument, about how she just needed to be in her own bed, with her own stuff, and that she would be fine tomorrow. But the words wouldn't come.

Cain turned her so they were standing face-to-face. She focused on his green eyes, using them as a lifeline to keep her from falling.

"Hays." He trailed a finger down her cheek. She wanted to lean into the softness of the touch, to the strength he offered. "You're about to fall over. I'll drive you."

"Fine. But I want to go to my apartment."

She saw his lips tighten as he glanced over at the smoldering building. "You need to stay with me. The fire inspector thinks, based on how fast the hallway burned, that whoever did this to the Bluewater was actually targeting you."

Chapter Six

Fourteen hours later, Cain sat in the living room of the house he'd grown up in sipping a cup of coffee, trying to tamp down the toxic blend of rage that surrounded him every time he thought of Hayley trapped in that fire.

He'd already done a thorough workout with the old set of free weights his dad kept in the garage. And had run five miles on the treadmill his mother had bought for walking after she'd had knee surgery.

Neither of those had really helped.

The longer Hayley slept up in his old bedroom, the worse the feelings became.

She was so damn exhausted that she had slept for fourteen goddamn hours.

Fourteen.

She'd been working on the computer codes while still trying to work double shifts at the Bluewater? Cain could feel his teeth grind and tried to force himself to relax. If he hadn't been called back to his office in DC—for a case completely unrelated—he would've been here and never allowed that to happen. Because Hayley had already been on the verge of collapse before taking on more work.

He rubbed his jaw.

He'd had his ear singed off by Ariel when he'd answered Hayley's phone, possibly the only dumbphone left in the world used by people under the age of eighty, when Ariel had called. Hayley had been so deeply asleep she hadn't even heard it ring over and over—seriously, he wasn't going to have any enamel left on his teeth by the end of this if he didn't chill out—so finally he'd answered it.

He'd explained to Ariel what happened. About the fire and danger Hayley might be in. About how she'd fallen so dead asleep on the way to his house that she hadn't heard her phone.

Ariel had pretty much told him to keep his distance from Hayley. Except with a lot more curse words and at a volume that rivaled a screaming jet engine. Guess she hadn't forgiven him for his part in Hayley's arrest.

His coffee wasn't helping his rage, but Cain knew he was going to have to channel it. Either that or have serious dental work done.

But more than that, he knew why he was holding on to his anger so tightly. Because it was much easier to handle the anger than the fear.

That moment of abject panic last night when he pulled up at the Bluewater, knowing Hayley was inside, and saw the flames.

Now it wasn't his jaw that clenched, it was his heart.

Thank God Hayley had the sense to beat on that can, otherwise Cain wouldn't have thought to look in the storage closet area. Wouldn't have been able to get her out.

The thought of losing Hayley… Cain put his coffee cup down on the table. One thing the fire had done was force him to take a good hard look at the truth. His feelings for Hayley hadn't died, no matter what had broken between them four years ago.

Catching the mole at Omega had really just been an excuse to bring him back into her life. If it hadn't been this, he would've found something else.

Cain had been waiting four years for Hayley to do her time so they could start again. He realized now that that had always been the truth. He had never planned to let her go.

Whatever secrets she was keeping from him, and he definitely knew they were there, he was going to find out.

And now it looked like he had brought danger to her door. Did the mole know what Cain was doing? If the fire inspector was correct and the hallway leading to the storage room had burned much quicker than it should have, then it looked like someone was deliberately targeting Hayley.

Of course, the fire inspector had also mentioned that it was possible that the hallway had traces of some nonsuspicious accelerants given that the storage room with its various chemicals was nearby. Just an unfortunate accident.

Either way, Cain didn't plan to be letting Hayley out of his sight. He didn't care much if Hayley or Ariel or the whole damn town didn't like that.

And keeping her safe wasn't the only reason he was going to be stuck to Hayley.

He'd received the code and key to release the ankle monitor that forced her to stay away from computers.

He'd made the decision late last night, especially since whatever she'd been working on had been lost in the fire, that Hayley was going to need access to a computer in order to discover information about the Omega mole. Going through reams of paper, especially if they had to start back at the beginning, would take too long.

Cain had submitted his request early this morning and it had been expedited to go before a local judge first thing, since a court order was needed to remove Hayley's ankle monitor.

He'd received the court order, the code needed to turn it off and the key—delivered by a state trooper—to remove the anklet all together. The condition of the court order was that Cain take responsibility for Hayley's computer activities. He was expected to know exactly what she was doing on any computer, and if she wasn't with him she would have the anklet back on.

That would not be a problem.

He was making lunch when Hayley finally woke up. She'd obviously taken a shower and slipped on a T-shirt and sweatpants of his that he'd left out for her.

The sight of her wearing his clothes did something to him. Grease popping from a piece of bacon brought his attention back to what he was doing.

"I pulled the sheets off the bed. I'm pretty sure they smelled like a flue. You should've made me take a shower before letting me sleep there."

"Believe it or not, I actually tried to wake you up. Short of dumping you in the cold shower myself, you were out."

And so damn exhausted he hadn't had it in him to force her back awake.

"I was tired."

The smallness of her voice kept him from lighting into her. He was back now. He wasn't going to let her work herself into the ground.

"Do you feel better?"

She reached her hands over her head in a giant stretch, arching her back. Thankfully bacon grease popped him again, or he might've started drooling.

"Oh my gosh, yes. I feel like my brain is working on all cylinders rather than only partial. You were right. I shouldn't have tried to do both jobs at the same time."

He took out the bacon and put on some eggs to fry. "Doesn't look like the Bluewater is even an option anymore. So let's say we just concentrate on your consultant work. Sit."

She raised an eyebrow but sat down at the table. He set a cup of coffee in front of her along with her much-needed cream and sugar.

"I was making progress before everything was lost." She rubbed her forehead as she took a sip of coffee. "I don't know how long it will take you to get another copy, but I'll try to remember where I was so I don't have to read through everything again."

When the eggs finished cooking he set a plate in front of her and sat down with his own.

"I'm going to actually do you one better. We're not going to use printouts. You're going to be on the computer."

She stuck her leg out from under the table, pointing to her ankle. "What about that?"

"Got the court order this morning that it can be turned and taken off as long as you're in my custody."

She didn't look as excited as he thought she would.

"Don't you still think this will all go much faster online rather than reading from the paper?" he asked as she nibbled on a piece of bacon.

"Yes." She nodded, but with a decided lack of enthusiasm. "Working your case from within the system will move much more quickly and intuitively for me."

"Then finish eating and let's get started."

HE BROUGHT THE laptop over to the couch where Hayley was sitting.

"You're only allowed on this while I'm sitting

right next to you. And we're only going to access the electronic versions of the files I brought, and possibly some outer Omega networks. Nothing else at all. Got it?"

Amazing how he had no problem trusting her within the Omega network. He didn't worry for a second that she would do anything damaging to any secrets the law enforcement agency might be protecting.

But that didn't mean he trusted her with any other aspect of a computer.

He knew she was keeping something from him, was in some sort of trouble or heading toward it, and he was handing her the tool to get in even deeper.

"Yes, I got it."

No smart-aleck remark, no teasing at all. He was glad she took this as seriously as he was.

As a matter fact, she almost looked scared as he handed the computer to her. As scared as she looked ten minutes ago when he turned off and removed her tracking anklet.

She sat with the computer on her lap, staring down at it for long moments, not touching it.

"Everything okay?" he finally asked.

"It's been a long time. I was in the cybercrimes wing at the correctional center, so there were no computers there. Nothing. Not even closed systems."

Computers not hooked to any other system so no damage could be done by viruses or hacks. No way in or out.

Guilt bubbled inside Cain. He had done this to her. Taking away something that had been a critical part of her.

Would he do anything differently if he could go back and change it?

He'd always thought not, because as the pithy saying went, she'd done the crime so she'd done the time. But looking at Hayley now, so awkwardly holding a computer that would've once been almost an appendage for her, hurt something inside him.

He touched her cheek with the back of his fingers. "Hays?"

She flinched and he dropped his hand. "Sorry. Yeah, let's get started."

Her fingers dropped to the keyboard and she began to work.

It didn't take long for her to get back into the flow of her talent. Hayley could write and develop and read computer code the way most people read nursery rhymes.

Cain wasn't nearly as good as Hayley, but he knew his way around coding, enough to be able to make sure she was staying within their agreed parameters.

She began her search scrolling through screen after screen of what would normally look like gibberish, stopping to follow different patterns that caught her eye.

Every time she found something suspicious she organized it into a separate folder. Once in a while she would take something out of a folder, evidently only after she'd been reassured that wasn't what she was looking for.

"Whoever is doing this is good," she said, standing up for the first time in four hours. She wiggled her fingers out in front of her, those muscles obviously sore after having not been used in that way for a long time.

"Better than you?"

She grinned. A smart-ass smile that he hadn't even realized had been missing until now. A smile full of confidence.

"Please. Don't insult me. I'll give it twenty-four hours before I find the pattern. *If* he's extremely lucky."

"Good." He grinned back at her. "How about if we take a break for a few minutes and I'll order us some dinner."

Her smile faded. "What time is it?"

"Almost five o'clock. You're not tired again, are you?" He said it in jest but then realized maybe she was tired. Maybe she did need more rest.

"No. But I've got to go."

"Go where?"

"Home. Just for a few hours. I can come back at around nine if you want. But right now I've got to go."

"Let's just stay and keep working. You were starting to get on a roll."

Her features became more pinched. "I'll have to pick it back up later."

Damn it. This had to do with whatever she was

hiding from him. Was she playing him? Had she somehow gotten a message out to someone while using the computer?

He looked down at her leg. Or maybe she thought to play him in a different way.

"That anklet is going right back on if you leave here for any reason."

She didn't get upset like he'd expected. Didn't try to talk her way out of it.

"That's fine."

He walked into the kitchen, true irritation kicking in, and snatched up the anklet. He stalked back into the living room.

"Foot," he demanded.

"Cain…" Her voice pleaded for understanding.

"Don't start. You were willing to work double shifts at that stupid restaurant and you won't even put in eight full hours of work to catch a killer?"

They both flinched as he snapped the monitor back in place around her slim ankle.

Her brown eyes stared out at him. "I just have something I need to do. I promise I'll be back in a few hours."

"You know this thing has a tracker, right? And now that I have the code, I'll be able to see where you're going?"

"I'm just going home. And yeah, if you feel like you need to track me go right ahead. You don't know me anymore. Don't know anything about my life."

He grabbed her arms, conscious not to hurt her. "Then tell me. Tell me what's happening with you."

All pleading was gone from her now. "Sorry, Cain, the great football star might be able to waltz back into the hearts of everyone else in town, but not mine. You and I are business, that's all."

She turned and left and he let her go, knowing going after her now would just make things worse.

But he damn well would use that tracker.

He grabbed the computer and began looking through the work she'd done today. Even after studying it nearly an hour he couldn't find anything at all suspicious. The only pattern he could find was the strides Hayley had made toward identifying the mole.

Maybe she just needed a break like she said. She was right—he didn't know anything about her life anymore.

That was an oversight he intended to rectify.

Chapter Seven

Hayley knew Cain was mad, and even understood his frustration, but she didn't care.

She was going home to see her son. She cursed when she got outside and realized she'd have to take a cab back to the Bluewater, where her car was still parked. But it would be worth it to have dinner with Mason, to read some of his stories he loved, to put him to bed.

She'd missed it for the last four days trying to work both jobs, but now that she had the time, she wouldn't miss it again. She'd lost too many "every-days" while she was in prison. She'd spend the rest of her life trying not to lose any more.

She told Cain she would come back at nine, and she would. She'd work all night if she needed to.

Although the thought of sitting on that couch with Cain a hair's breadth away caused heat to pool in her very core.

Maybe it was all the sleep, maybe it was work-ing in the house that held so many memories for her, maybe it was not having sex for the last four years. But she was so aware of Cain, of the musky scent of him, of his strength and broody intelligence.

It had been all she could do most of the afternoon to concentrate on the coding and not put the computer aside and crawl on top of him.

Her mind and her heart wanted to stay far away from him, but her body had much different ideas. She tried to remind her body that he'd used their relationship, their history, to get close to her and then arrest her.

Still hadn't seemed to make much difference.

Good thing Hayley was used to her body not getting what it wanted. She'd had four years of desperately wanting things she couldn't have. A few days with Cain Bennett shouldn't be a problem.

All thoughts of Cain melted away after she made it to her car then drove to her apartment. She let herself in and heard Mason's sweet voice chattering to Ariel.

"What's going on in here?"

"Mama Hayley! Yay!" Mason ran and launched himself at her. She snatched him up in her arms, swinging him around as she hugged him and he giggled. The sweetest sound she'd ever heard.

"Guess what?" She tapped him on the nose as she set him back down on the ground. "I got to see some real live fire trucks last night."

Mason's eyes got huge. "You did?"

The three of them made a pizza together, each of

them putting on whatever toppings they wanted, as Hayley told a very tame version of the restaurant fire and the fire trucks. Mason asked all sorts of questions, stating more than once that he was going to be a fireman when he grew up. She could tell Ariel had adult questions, but neither of them would talk about that in front of Mason.

After dinner they watched an episode of Mason's favorite show together, then colored a couple of pictures. Mason drew his own version of a fire truck.

Before Hayley knew it, it was already time to get her little man ready for bed. She gave him a bath, read him his stories—all more than once—before tucking him in.

"Tomorrow's Wednesday." His grin was overpowered by a yawn.

"Hmmm. Wednesday, Wednesday." She pursed her lips to the side and tapped them. "There's something I'm supposed to remember about Wednesday, but I can't think what it is."

"Ice cream Wednesday!" Mason yelled. "We always get ice cream on Wednesday."

Hayley smiled and tickled him, but stopped before he could get wound up. "Oh yeah, that's right. Of course we're going to get ice cream tomorrow. It's Wednesday."

It had been their tradition every week since Hayley had come home. She wouldn't be breaking it tomorrow, although getting away from Cain in the middle of the afternoon would require some creative strategizing.

"I love you, little man. Sweet dreams."

"Night, Mama." His eyes were already drifting closed, which was good—he wouldn't see the tears flooding hers.

Mama, not Mama Hayley. One day that would be what he said all the time, not just as he was falling asleep.

Ariel was washing dishes when Hayley came back out. Hayley took over the drying duties.

"I'm glad you're okay. I talked to Cain Bennett twice last night, first time when he came over here looking for you, second when I called you and he finally answered. He said you were so deeply asleep that you weren't even hearing your phone ring."

Hayley winced. She had texted Ariel from the Bluewater, not wanting her to hear about the fire on the news and worry. She'd meant to call later with more details. "Yeah, if you called I didn't hear it at all."

Hayley filled her in. Stuff they hadn't been able to say in front of Mason. By the end of it, Ariel was staring at Hayley wide-eyed.

"It's a damn good thing Cain came by to find you. You could've died!"

Hayley could still feel the heat of the fire, the suffocating smoke. "Believe me, I know."

Ariel let the dishwater out of the sink. "He was pretty mad when he found out you were trying to do both jobs."

Hayley grimaced. "It seemed like a good idea at the time. Speaking of, I've got to get back there. We're starting to make some actual progress."

Hayley dried the baking pan and put it away.

"You're going to have to tell him, Hayley," Ariel said softly.

Hayley froze midaction, but respected her cousin too much to pretend she didn't know what Ariel was talking about.

"How long have you known?"

"I didn't realize it until he showed up here yesterday, although I should have. Cain Bennett has always been the one for you."

He'd been the *only* one her whole life. The only man she'd ever been with, the only man she ever loved.

She gripped the towel in her hand, not looking at Ariel. "I can't tell him. I'm scared. I'm scared I'll lose Mason."

"Just because you have a criminal record does not mean a judge would give Cain custody of Mason, even if he tried to take him. You have no history of violence, drug abuse or neglect. If anything, we could prove how you very methodically planned for Mason's future by making me guardian when he was born."

Hayley sighed. "It's not just that. There are some other things that are…complicated. Things that have nothing to do with Cain."

She didn't want to give Ariel too much information about the people who might come after Hayley. The more Ariel knew, the more dangerous it could be for her.

Hayley's hacking—selling fake college entrance test scores to rich kids—had been pretty benign compared to what she'd stumbled across when she'd been trying to get out.

Someone was using the CET exam to commit treason. To sell government state secrets to other countries. Someone with a lot of political power.

The only thing that had kept Hayley alive so far was that she didn't know *who* that someone was. She'd been arrested before she could dig deep enough.

But Hayley had the means of discovering who. As soon as she had free rein of a computer she would be able to access the electronic trapdoor she'd planted in the CET system before she was arrested.

But once she accessed it, whoever was behind the scheme would know she knew. If they'd already found it, they might suspect her even now.

Either way, she had to be ready to run if it came down to it.

"I know there's trouble you're not telling me about, coz," Ariel said softly. "I know that's why you've been working so hard, not just so that I could go to Oxford."

She'd done her best to protect Ariel, but she should've known her cousin was too smart not to suspect something else was going on.

"The less you know about it the better."

Ariel nodded. "I'm sure that's true. But what about Cain? Whatever trouble you're in, he can help. He has the resources."

"He was the person who arrested me in the first place."

Ariel's lips tightened. "Trust me, I'm never going to forgive what he did, especially now that I know that he must have slept with you right before he arrested you, but I also know that he will help. He will protect you from whatever it is you're afraid of. Especially if he knows about Mason."

Would he? Would Cain even believe her if she tried to explain? She wouldn't know if her computer trap had worked unless she got online. And even once she did, there was no guarantee that it would still be there. She didn't think it would've been discovered deep in the network where she'd placed it, but it was possible.

There was no way Cain was just going to take her word that there had been more involved in her hacker case than he thought. He would think she was using him to gain access to a computer.

So she would have to bide her time. Make sure there were no traces of her presence online while she did the consulting work for Cain. She would deal with the trapdoor and its ramifications once her parole was over and she had full access to computers again. And she'd be ready to take Mason and run if she needed to. Ariel would at least be across the ocean studying.

And she would make sure Cain didn't find out about Mason. At one time she would've given anything for their lives to be tied together with a child. But he'd made his choice, decided he didn't want a permanent link with her, four years ago.

Telling him about Mason would just complicate matters. And God knew everything was already complicated enough as it was.

Chapter Eight

Cain woke up on the couch with Hayley sprawled on top of him. Caught in that place between wakefulness and dreams, his mind sighed in contentment. It felt so good to hold her again.

He stretched, shifting slightly, pulling her closer. His thigh slid between hers and his arms extended more tightly around her, one hand splayed on her hip, the other arm around her shoulders.

Hayley stretched, too, rubbing against him, almost purring. Cain just pulled her closer.

They'd always slept like this, as if they couldn't get close enough in sleep, the way they always felt like they couldn't get close enough when they were awake. Of course, there hadn't been an abundance of opportunities to sleep all night together, first because of high school and parents, then because of the physical distance between them in college, and then because Hayley had gone…

Cain's eyes flew open, now completely aware of where he was and what was happening.

But he couldn't force himself to let go of Hayley.

They'd worked well into the night after she returned yesterday evening. He sat next to her on the couch as she continued her search. He'd been even more diligent to make sure she wasn't communicating with anyone else while doing this work.

He knew, like she'd said, that she had just gone home when she'd left him yesterday. But that didn't mean that someone couldn't have met her there. Cain had made a mistake in not following her, surveilling her apartment, seeing what she was up to.

He wouldn't make that mistake again.

She'd made progress in her work here, he knew she had. Had pinpointed a pattern in how the Omega traitor was communicating. And although Hayley didn't know what it meant, when she'd shown him the origin of the communications, Cain's heart had taken a dive.

It looked like the mole was someone inside the SWAT team at Omega sector. He prayed they were wrong. And he definitely wouldn't make any accusations until they had proof. Hayley would find it soon.

Somewhere around 4:00 a.m., when she'd started to nod off, he'd taken the laptop from her and laid it on the table. He planned for both of them to go to their separate rooms, separate beds, but hadn't wanted to be forced to put that damn anklet back on her.

But unless he planned to stay up all night guarding her, there was no way he could take the chance of letting her sneak by him while he slept.

He leaned back on the couch, about to explain what needed to happen, when he heard her cute little snore. He didn't have the heart to wake her up.

Instead he had pulled Hayley down on the couch and tucked her into his side. Which at some point had obviously turned into entangled limbs and Hayley on top of him.

But right now all Cain wanted to do was keep her pulled up against him. Let her body get the sleep it still obviously needed.

He dozed, too, and it was midmorning when he awoke, Hayley still in his arms. He knew the second she woke up, too. Or, at least the second she realized exactly where she was lying.

She went from soft and purring and snuggly to ramrod straight, pushing herself partway up with her hands on his chest so she could look into his eyes.

"I fell asleep." Her eyes were blinking rapidly as she tried to figure out exactly what was happening.

"I noticed."

She tried to sit up, but their limbs were so tangled she couldn't quite manage.

"Are you going to let me go?"

Cain tucked an arm under his head. "I haven't decided."

His fingers splayed more widely on her hip and almost of their own accord began rubbing gentle circles.

She eased her weight back down on top of him. "What are you doing?"

"Do you remember this couch?"

Oh, the trouble they had gotten into on this couch in high school.

"I remember always having to keep an ear out for the front door opening," she said. He could hear the smile in her voice. "And very quickly rearranging clothing."

His parents had come home more than once at an inopportune moment. "Yeah, they had impeccable timing, didn't they?"

Hayley lifted her head up to make some comment, but he kissed her before she could. It was almost like he couldn't control his own body.

Their kisses had always been wildly passionate and engulfing. This was no different. As soon as his lips touched hers, he used his arm around her hips to pull her more fully up against him. His other hand wrapped around the back of her neck.

He kissed the side of her mouth, running his tongue over her lower lip, then drew back just a fraction of an inch before plunging back deep inside her hot, wet mouth. He felt her hands tangle into his hair, keeping him as close as he was keeping her.

He tilted her head to the side, giving his lips access to her jaw, her throat. Heard her moan as he made his way down that feminine curve with gentle bites soothed by soft flicks of his tongue.

A loud beeping noise—*that wouldn't quit, damn it*—on the computer brought Cain back to his senses.

"That's the alarm from the algorithm I set up to run while I was offline to see if we could spot a specific pattern," Hayley said against his lips.

The words threw cold water on his ardor. His hand on her nape now pulled her away rather than pulling her closer.

"You did what?"

Unease flared in her eyes. "It's just a simple pattern recognition program I set up to run. Mostly for elimination purposes. There was no point in me doing it manually. This way was much quicker."

It made sense. Was reasonable. But what pissed Cain off was that he'd had no idea she'd done it. Had no idea she'd set up a program to run.

"When did you do it?" He slid back from her.

She sat up, pulling away. "I don't know, a little while after we figured out the communication pattern I showed you last night. We agreed I needed to focus on where that pattern was occurring, so that's what I did."

"But you didn't tell me you set up a program to do it."

She shrugged. "I wasn't trying to hide it from you. I didn't plant the program within the Omega system if that's what you're worried about. It's running right here on your laptop."

"That's not the problem."

"Then what is the problem? I'm trying to do what you asked me to do in the most efficient way possible." She flung her blond hair over her shoulder and slid even farther from him on the couch.

"I just didn't know what you were doing."

He'd sat by her the entire night and hadn't recognized that she'd built the program to help her. If she could do *that* without him knowing, how much more difficult could it be for her to make contact with her hacker buddies without him knowing it?

She arched her eyebrow. "I didn't realize I needed to explain every step of what I was doing. I just thought we were trying to catch your killer as quickly as possible."

"And what else are you trying to sneak by me while you have access to a computer and I obviously have no idea what you're doing?" Cain crossed his arms over his chest, watching her closely, looking for lies.

Her eyes narrowed. "What the hell are you talking about? I haven't been doing anything. You've been peeking over my shoulder the whole time."

"Are you telling me I don't need to?"

"I'm telling you I'm doing the job you're paying me to do."

"But we both know that it wouldn't be difficult for you to squeeze in a little extra contact with someone else if I'm not watching. Hell, even if I *am* watching, as proven today."

Her lips flattened into a thin line. "I haven't done a single thing that didn't involve Omega Sector. Not one single thing."

"You'll have to excuse me if I don't believe you, given the obvious secrets you've been trying to keep."

Her face paled, and he knew he was definitely on the right track.

"Damn it, Hayley, I don't want you to get back in trouble. Didn't you learn anything the first time?"

Hayley stood up and walked toward the kitchen. "Yeah, I learned that the person I thought I could trust the most slept with me so he could make a big arrest to further his career."

He stood up. "That's not true."

"You know what? It doesn't matter." She rubbed her hand against her forehead as if a headache was forming. "Let's get something to eat and get back to work. My evil program has obviously discovered a pattern. Something that would've taken me days to find on my own."

Cain grimaced. She was right. They needed to focus. Their personal stuff could wait until they caught the traitor.

"Fine." He walked into the kitchen, started the coffeepot and made sandwiches.

"You want me to bring the computer in here to work?"

Cain grimaced. He obviously needed to watch her more closely while she was on it. He couldn't do that while he was making brunch.

"No. Just wait till after we eat."

His words were a blatant announcement of how

much he didn't trust her. He saw her small shoulders go rigid before giving a stiff nod.

"Fine." Tension radiated in the word. "I've got to leave at three o'clock for a few hours, so let's hurry up and get this done."

She was leaving *again*? The evening yesterday and then the afternoon today? This was more than just time off to hang out with Ariel. He wanted to argue, demand to know where she was going, but knew she wouldn't tell him. Arguing with Hayley now would just make things more difficult between them.

And outside of using a computer or breaking any other conditions of her parole, she was free to do what she wanted. Cain couldn't stop her.

His fist clenched around the coffeepot handle. No, he couldn't stop her if she was going off somewhere to meet one of her hacker cronies.

He really couldn't stop her if she was determined to slide back into that life. He could stop her now, but soon, probably in the next couple of weeks the way she was sorting through the data concerning the mole, Cain wouldn't be here to harass her into making good choices. He didn't want to believe that she wanted the life of a criminal. The Hayley he'd known—and loved—would never have wanted that.

Maybe the Hayley he'd known in high school was well and truly gone. Something in his soul shattered at the thought.

They never had a chance to talk about why she

started hacking. Why she hadn't stayed in college and gotten a real job afterward. Hayley had never been lazy, had never just wanted to take the easiest way.

But Cain didn't ask now. They just finished their meal in silence.

Afterward she brought the computer to the kitchen table, obviously wanting distance from the couch. She explained everything she was doing without him having to ask. He appreciated it, but it took a lot of time. Slowed her down significantly.

And at some point, when she was talking to him and still typing full speed at the same time, he realized the truth.

"You don't have to tell me what you're doing," he said. "I know that slows you down. Just do the work."

She relaxed just slightly. "You trust that I'm only working on the Omega Sector case?"

Cain shook his head, feeling like a jerk, even though his words were the truth.

"No. I've just realized that even while explaining something to me, you could still be slipping in or accessing something completely different if you wanted to. So trust is a moot point."

WHEN SHE LEFT at three o'clock, he followed.

He hadn't given her a hard time about leaving, which worked out well seeing as they hadn't really spoken except for work-related questions since their midmorning meal. She told him she would be back before nightfall and he just nodded.

They both flinched again as he reconnected her ankle monitor.

As soon as she walked out the door he went to the computer and turned on the tracking feature. Then got in his car with the computer.

Maybe she was just going home again. If so, fine. But if anybody else showed up at her apartment he was going to know about it.

He refused to give in to his thoughts earlier today that Hayley was beyond saving. She wasn't. She may be on the road to trouble again, but damn it, not on his watch. Not this time. If she needed money he would help her. If she needed a job he would help her.

She wasn't on drugs; she didn't have any elaborate lifestyle. How bad off could she really be?

When the tracker showed her car had driven past her apartment his lips pursed. This didn't change anything. Just made him more determined.

When her car had stopped at what looked like a restaurant, Cain sped up. This was some sort of meeting. Anger clenched in his stomach. Fear that he wouldn't be able to take care of Hayley, to get her out of whatever mess she was getting herself into, was closing in right behind the anger.

As he arrived he saw it wasn't a restaurant but the local fast-food ice-cream joint. He pulled his car to the far side of the parking lot and watched. Hayley hadn't even gotten out of her car yet.

Maybe he should go get her now. Stop whatever was about to happen before it could even start.

He was opening his door when he saw another car pull up next to Hayley's. Then watched, somewhat dumbfounded, as Ariel got out of the other car. She opened the back seat door, reached in and pulled out a little boy.

Cain felt like the biggest jackass on the planet. Hayley was meeting her cousin and her—what? Nephew? Second cousin?—for a midafternoon ice-cream break.

He scrubbed a hand over his face. He'd been so busy looking for nefarious reasons why Hayley would need money and be sneaking away that he hadn't taken into consideration that she truly might have *good* reasons. Like helping her cousin, who'd obviously had a baby while Hayley was in prison, with living expenses. Hayley and Ariel had always been as close as sisters. Not being there for Ariel when she needed Hayley would've weighed heavily on Hayley. Maybe she was trying to make up for that now.

The kid, who was two or maybe three years old, obviously loved both women. He gave Hayley a huge hug before she picked him up and they walked into the ice-cream place together. He watched them for a few more seconds with his binoculars.

Cain wanted to join them. Wished he had the right to join them. Maybe if he hadn't been such an ass to her today she would've invited him along.

She wasn't in trouble and in need of being rescued. She was just trying to rebuild her life after a pretty harsh blow.

He watched them much longer than he should have, even knowing he looked like a creepy stalker. But Hayley's face was so lit up and happy he couldn't stop watching. It made him aware of how tense she was around him.

He watched the kid bite a huge chunk out of the bottom of his cone and both women jump to grab napkins as ice cream started running out the bottom. Cain chuckled. He and his brother had done the same thing as kids, driving his parents crazy.

The boy sucked the ice cream out of the bottom of his cone, then wiggled and squirmed as Hayley tried to wipe his face. He said something that obviously made her laugh.

Cain was about to put his binoculars away, since there obviously was no danger to national security here, when Hayley pulled the kid in for a hug, her fingers threading in his slightly-too-long hair at the nape of his neck, lifting it.

A dark brown birthmark about an inch in diameter could be seen before she let him go and his hair fell back in place, covering it.

Cain felt like all the air had been sucked out of his car.

He had a birthmark just like that at the exact same place on his neck.

Chapter Nine

Cain started his car and drove back to his house in a daze. His brain struggled to do the math. It wasn't possible that Hayley had a child, was it?

He was on the phone to Ren McClement in the Omega DC office, the only other person besides Steve Drackett who knew what was going on, before he even got inside the house. He needed info he couldn't get himself in case it led the mole to them.

"What's up, Cain? Any progress? Didn't expect to hear from you so soon."

"Ren, I need you to do something for me personally." Cain skipped any sort of greeting.

"Yes," Ren said immediately. No stipulations, just whatever Cain needed. Sign of a true friend. "Tell me."

"I need you to check Hayley Green's medical records from the first year she was in prison."

"I'm pulling them up now. Anything in particular I'm looking for?"

"You'll know it when you see it. Trust me."

"It's running. Hayley is the same Hayley Green

that we got the court order for yesterday, right? The one you're working with?"

"Yeah." Cain paced as he waited for Ren to access the info.

"Okay, I've got the records. Looks like she… Oh my gosh."

Cain closed his eyes. "Tell me."

"Baby boy was born five months after Hayley arrived at the Georgia Women's Correctional Institute. No father listed on the birth certificate. Custody given to an Ariel Green upon birth of child."

Hayley had given birth to a baby, Cain's baby. In jail. Oh dear God.

"Cain? You okay? I don't want to pry, but…"

Cain blew out a breath. "Yeah, looks like this case just got a little more complicated."

"Um, are congratulations in order?"

Cain's short bark of laughter held very little humor. "It would seem so. I haven't talked to her about it, so I don't know much more than the fact that the kid has the exact same birthmark in the exact same place I do."

"That's a pretty sure sign."

"I'll let you know if this changes anything for the case. Thanks, Ren. I owe you one."

"Nah, brother, that one's a freebie for sure."

Cain stared at nothing for a long time after he got off the phone, trying to remember all the details from four years ago.

How the hell could he have not known Hayley was pregnant?

The case had been expedited, thanks to public scrutiny of the CET exam, led mostly by Senator Ralph Nelligar. Under normal circumstances her cybercrime case might have sat for months before being heard by a jury. Hayley would've been in a county holding cell and there would've been no way she could've kept him in the dark about the baby.

But once a US senator was involved things had moved along much more quickly. Then, Hayley had pleaded no contest at her arraignment, eliminating the need for a longer trial. By the time she was at the Georgia Women's Correctional, she was probably four months pregnant. Not quite showing if someone wasn't looking for it.

Cain definitely hadn't been looking for it.

He began pacing back and forth, his fingers going to the birthmark on his neck. No wonder she'd refused to see him when he'd visited her the first year. After that he'd kept tabs on her, made sure she hadn't run into any trouble or had any health issues, but had thought it better not to try to see her.

How could she have not told him? How could he have missed this?

He was furious. With her. With himself. With the entire situation.

But part of him was relieved that he at least now knew her secret. Knew why she'd been sneaking around. Was thrilled that she wasn't falling back into hacking.

But he was still furious.

When Hayley arrived back at his house a couple hours later, Cain had gotten himself under control. Yelling wasn't going to accomplish anything.

Although exactly what Cain hoped to accomplish he wasn't sure at all.

"Cain?" Hayley called out as she entered through the door.

Most of the lights were off in the house. "I'm in the kitchen."

She looked more relaxed, looser, than she had before she left. She stopped in the hallway, not quite all the way into the eating area where he sat.

"Feeling better?" he asked. "Good break?"

"Yeah. Ready to get to it." She took a step closer. "Look, I'm sorry about before. I will explain everything more clearly. Show you what I'm doing so you don't have to be worried that it's something on the computer I'm not supposed to."

Oh, they had much different problems to worry about now.

"Sit down."

She sat opposite him, holding out her foot for him to remove the anklet. Instead he slid the photo album he'd placed on the table toward her.

Hayley smiled as she looked down at the twenty-five-year-old pictures.

"Oh my gosh, is that your mom? Look at that hair!"

His smile didn't reach his eyes. "I know. Styles have changed a lot since then."

"What's the matter, Bennett? You have so much time on your hands that you had to go reminiscing?"

He flipped the page over and pointed to a particular picture. "Actually, this was the picture I was studying. Wanted to show you."

It was one someone had taken of him when he was about three. His dad was ruffling his hair, which made the birthmark—the exact one he'd seen on the little boy today—more noticeable.

She looked back and forth between him and the picture, color leaching from her face. She slid her chair back farther from him and stood, looking like she might bolt at any second.

"Wh-why are you showing me that picture?"

He wasn't going to beat around the bush. "I know about the boy, Hayley."

All remaining color left. She gripped the back of the chair like she might fall over. "How?"

"I thought you were trying to get back in touch with your hacker friends. That's why I was so suspicious about all the work you were doing for me."

Confusion was clear on her face. "I wasn't."

"When you wanted to leave yesterday, I was convinced you were meeting someone. The same this afternoon."

"You followed me," she whispered.

He nodded. "My intentions were good. I wanted to see what I could do to help. Even had binoculars to watch you. I wanted to keep you away from whatever big baddies you were meeting. The big baddies ended up being Ariel and what I thought was her son."

Hayley stared down at the ground.

"But it wasn't Ariel's son, I realized, when I saw the birthmark. It only took a phone call to confirm that you gave birth in prison. That you are the mother of *my* son."

Hayley didn't look at him. "His name is Mason. He's three and a half."

Mason.

"How could you not have told me about him?" He slammed his fist against the table.

She looked back up at him, heat in her cheeks. "When was I supposed to do that, Cain? We weren't exactly speaking to each other at the time."

"You should've made the effort."

"You'd made it abundantly clear how little I'd meant to you."

He rolled his eyes. "Because I had you arrested for a crime you actually committed?"

"No. Because you slept with me knowing you were going to be arresting me a few days later. You used the feelings you knew I had for you to get information to put me in jail." Now she slammed her hand on the table. "So yeah, I took that to mean you didn't really care about me very much."

Her words doused his righteous fire. God, was that what she really thought? That he'd gone to bed with her four years ago because he wanted to use that to entrap her?

"Hayley." The anger had fled from his tone now. "I'll admit when we discovered the hacker network involved with selling the CET answers, I came to you. But not because I planned to arrest you."

Disbelief sat clear on her features.

"When I first contacted you, I had no idea you were involved. I'll admit I planned to use you as a source, but I didn't know you were actually one of the hackers until later. By then we were already together."

He—as always—hadn't been able to stay away from her. They'd been drawn to each other like magnets just like they had been in high school.

He'd stopped it, stayed away, when he'd realized she was one of the people his team would be arresting. But the wheels were already in motion and Cain couldn't stop it. He'd spent the night before the bust getting piss drunk, so furious that he couldn't do anything to protect Hayley without compromising everything he'd sworn to uphold as a law enforcement officer.

It had ripped his guts out.

"I was pretty damn mad at you when I found out what you'd done. Couldn't believe you'd be that stupid." He stared into her brown eyes. "But I never initiated contact with you with the intent to arrest you."

The opposite. If he'd found out early enough to help her get out of the situation completely before

Omega's cybercrime division had gotten on her trail, he probably would've done it.

She just shook her head. "Yeah, well, it didn't look that way from where I was sitting in the handcuffs."

HE KNEW. Cain finally knew.

Anger, frustration, pain, were radiating off him from across the table. Hayley knew she'd see the same in her features if she looked in the mirror.

But under it all she felt relief. He *knew*.

"I was so angry," she told him. "But also afraid. I didn't know what to do. What was going to happen to me or the baby. I thought you had used me to further your career, to make a name for yourself or whatever."

"You thought I would deny the baby was mine."

She turned away, couldn't even bear to look at him. "I thought I was just a girl from your past who you discovered was doing something illegal. So you slept with me to get close. Plus, I thought if I started making a lot of noise about getting knocked up from one of my arresting officers I might get in even more trouble."

She'd seen the look in his eyes that day in the courtroom. He hadn't seemed angry or even cold. He'd seemed so *disappointed* in her. She'd been disappointed enough in herself. So as weak as it made her seem, she hadn't wanted to get him in trouble, either.

She heard a low curse from across the table. "Damn it, Hayley, *why*?"

What other reason could she give him? "I—"

"Not the baby, although I want to know everything there is to know about him. Tell me why you ended up in my pathway to begin with. Why were you involved with something illegal?"

His words were so heartfelt, so desperate, she felt whatever anger she had left melt out of her.

"My dad got sick. Cancer." She sat down at the table across from Cain. "I had a year left in college when I had to come back home and take care of him. You know how it is, never enough money. His insurance was pitiful."

God, it sounded like such a cop-out. It had to, especially to Cain, the one who had grown up with such a crystal clear sense of right and wrong, black-and-white. He'd always known he wanted to work in law enforcement.

"I was working at the Bluewater, but couldn't make ends meet. A friend of mine I'd gone to school with asked if I wanted to do some freelance stuff."

"Kenneth Vargas."

She nodded. "It seemed like an answer to prayer. Jobs I could do from home and still be able to take care of my dad.

"For about six months he paid me pretty well to do some legit computer jobs." She rubbed her hands across her eyes. "Ends up those jobs were really auditions. When he realized what I could really do, how pretty desperate I was, he mentioned another possibility that would completely take care of my financial woes. Kenneth was a good salesman. Said we wouldn't be hurting anyone. Selling CET results to rich little brats."

The test itself couldn't be hacked, but the results and reporting system could. But it involved programming and had to be done manually each time to avoid detection.

Ended up Vargas was using a dozen other people with Hayley's skills from all over the country. His greed had made the hacks much more noticeable.

"I'll be honest, I didn't need much convincing from Vargas. I liked the challenge of it and it got me the money I needed."

She looked across the table, but not directly at Cain. Didn't want to see further disappointment in his eyes.

"I don't know if you care or if you'll even believe me, but I was already getting out when the arrest went down. Had taken part in fewer and fewer hacks."

She saw Cain wipe a hand over his face and chanced a glance at him. "That's probably why you didn't show up in my initial suspects list," he said. "I knew you went to school with Vargas, knew him. But I didn't know you were a part of the group we were about to arrest."

Knowing he hadn't slept with her in order to arrest her changed a lot for Hayley. At least it didn't make her feel like he cared nothing about her, that their connection hadn't meant nothing to him.

She shrugged. "Like you said, I was guilty. Re-gardless of whether I was getting out of it or not, I had committed the crime."

Her father had died and the desperate need for money had passed. Once the panic had been gone, she'd realized what she was doing. Had been ashamed.

If she'd gotten out just one month earlier her life would've been totally different. One month would've probably kept her off Cain's radar. She probably never would've gone to jail.

And, maybe even more importantly, if she'd got-ten out one month earlier she would've never stum-bled on to the information that might one day cost her her life.

Someone was using the CET exam at international Department of Defense schools, to sell state secrets. Hayley had discovered the when, where and how, and had been in the process of finding out who when she'd been arrested and banned from computers.

Cain leaned in closer to her. "I never dreamed the judge would sentence you for as long as he did. I thought he would take into consideration your lack of criminal record. I honestly never thought you would go to prison. Especially not for four years."

She just shrugged. "It was a high-profile case. Besides, would it have really made any difference in your decision to arrest me? I was the bad guy."

He stared at her for a long moment. "Maybe. I…" He trailed off, then finally shrugged. "Maybe."

"I'm sorry I didn't tell you about Mason. I was

angry and scared and honestly thought you were completely done with me. Would not want to be associated with me at all, even in this way. I was a criminal. How could you possibly want me after that?"

They stared at each other across the table for a long time, most of the truth finally open between them. She wished she could tell him the rest, but she couldn't. Not without proof.

His green eyes held her captive as he leaned closer. "I think there's one thing you better get clear. I have never stopped wanting you."

Chapter Ten

Hours later, Cain sat on the same couch where he'd woken up that morning, but this time Hayley very definitely wasn't in his arms. They'd talked more before finally reaching some sort of emotional truce and had begun working. They had finally decided to stop when Hayley announced she would probably need to access the Omega servers on-site to definitely be sure about what she was seeing.

Cain's anger had eased. It was impossible to stay mad when he forced himself to look at the situation from Hayley's point of view.

They'd both been wrong. Both made bad choices. The past couldn't be changed, but the future wasn't yet written.

He had a son.

He wanted to rush in and force himself into Mason's life. To get to know him. But Cain realized Hayley was also just getting to know the little boy. That she'd lost just as much time as Cain had. More.

He had no doubt after watching Hayley interact

with Mason today that she loved the child. Wanted what was best for him. Cain did, too.

So he could wait. Ease himself into the child's life. But he would be part of it, no matter what he had to do.

He looked down at Hayley, tucked on the opposite side of the couch. He wanted to be part of her life, too. She'd always been important to him, even in the years they were separated while they were in college and then while he was pursuing his law enforcement dreams.

It was why what he'd seen as her betrayal hurt so much. How could she have broken the law when upholding it had always been so important to him? Hearing her explanation helped. Knowing she took responsibility for the choices she'd made helped even more.

But even in the tentative peace they'd made last night, both of them not knowing exactly what to do with it, Hayley seemed to have more secrets. Were the shadows in her eyes because of what had happened in the past? Because part of Cain was afraid there was something she was still hiding from him.

A hand slamming on his front door had Hayley jerking awake and Cain heading toward the door. He grabbed his sidearm on the kitchen counter out of habit.

Cain cracked open the door. Damn. The Georgia state troopers standing on his porch were not who he was expecting at all. And not who he wanted to face with a gun in his hand.

Cain nodded at them, keeping his sidearm behind the door. "Officers."

One of the officers held up a piece of paper. "We have a warrant for the arrest of Hayley Green for violation of her parole. Intel indicated that she was inside this house."

What the hell?

"There's been some mistake. I'm federal law enforcement, and I was given a court order allowing the easement of Ms. Green's parole restrictions, specifically concerning her use of computers."

"Is Ms. Green in the house, sir?" the second cop asked.

"Look, just let me get my badge and the court order."

Cop One stuck his hand out to stop Cain from closing the door. "Is Ms. Green in the house?"

Damn it. This was about to get out of hand.

"She is." Cain looked from one man to the other. "Also, you should be warned that I'm currently holding a firearm."

The tension in the cops skyrocketed as Cain lowered the hand holding the gun hidden behind the door. He kept it very loosely by his side, trying to show he meant no harm.

As he'd been afraid of, Cain's lack of threat didn't seem to matter to these guys. Both had their weapons drawn and pointed at him.

Cop One took a step back. "Hands up in the air. Right now."

Cain raised them, keeping his hand over the muzzle of the gun rather than at the trigger. He hoped they could see there was no way he could shoot them like this. But tensions were high with police officers all over the country. No cop wanted to take a chance with a stranger with a gun in his hand.

"I'm going to hand this to you, all right?" Both of these troopers were young. Cain didn't want to give them any excuse to use excessive force. "Then I will get my law enforcement credentials and we can work this out."

"Cain, what's going on?"

Cop One threw the door open wide at Hayley's words and aimed his firearm at her. Guy looked a little nervous. "Get your hands up! Do you have a gun?" he demanded of Hayley, although with both hands empty it seemed obvious she didn't.

"No." Hayley raised her arms, getting paler by the second. "What's going on?"

Cop Two, a little more calm than his buddy, turned to her. "Are you Hayley Green?"

Hayley nodded.

"We have a warrant for your arrest, for violation of your parole."

Cain could feel her eyes on him. "Cain?"

Damn it, her voice sounded so scared.

He gave her the most reassuring smile he could muster. "We're going to get this worked out."

He turned to the officers. "Look, what's your name?" he said to the more calm one.

"Perowne."

"I'm Cain Bennett. I work for Omega Sector, federal law enforcement. Hayley Green is my authorized consultant for a case. Like I said, I have a court order giving her temporary freedom from her tracking anklet."

"I understand that, sir, but that's going to have to be addressed down at central booking. Our instructions were to bring her in."

The other guy strode past Cain, weapon still raised, and turned Hayley forcefully against the hallway wall. "Put your hands on the wall and spread your legs."

The guy wasn't brutal, but he definitely wasn't gentle as he pushed Hayley's chest into the wall with a hand on her shoulder blades as he put his sidearm back into its holster.

Frustration burned through Cain as he saw a tear fall down Hayley's terrified face. The cop jerked back one of her arms, then the other, cuffing them.

"Be cool, Brickman," Perowne muttered.

"You just keep your eye on supercop over there." Brickman began reading Hayley her rights as he ran his hands up her legs to make sure she wasn't hiding any weapons, then patted down her sides and chest.

Another tear fell, all color gone from her face completely. Cain was actually afraid she might faint.

"Hayley, it's okay. We're going to get this worked out. Do you hear me?"

She nodded just slightly.

Short of violently disarming the cops, which Cain might've done if it wouldn't have put Hayley at risk, there was nothing he could do. Although it went against every protective grain in his body, Cain was going to have to let them take her.

Brickman continued to use a hand on Hayley's shoulder to keep her pushed up against the wall while he turned to Cain. It was a punk move just to show his power.

It took all of Cain's considerable willpower not to show Brickman just how precious his position of power really was when he heard Hayley's soft whimper.

"Cut it out, Paul," Perowne said. "Take her to the car."

Cain touched Hayley's arm as the officer walked her by. "I'll be right behind you."

"If you can show me your credentials, I can give this back to you." Perowne holstered his own weapon and lifted Cain's.

Cain got his ID from the counter and showed it to the other man, along with the court order.

Perowne handed him back his gun. "Agent Bennett, I'm sorry for the misunderstanding. And that court order looks official, so I don't know exactly what the problem is. Like I said, if you can come to the courthouse, hopefully you can get everything worked out."

Cain handed the man Hayley's anklet. "You'll need this."

The cop just nodded and they walked outside together. Cain could see Hayley fighting back tears from the back seat of the squad car, her arms at an awkward angle thanks to the cuffs.

He wasn't letting her return to jail. Watching her go the first time, even when he'd known she'd been guilty, had taken everything he had. There was no way he was letting it happen now.

FEAR WAS A fist in Hayley's throat, blocking her airway. She tried to think through the panic. This was just a misunderstanding. Some sort of paperwork glitch. Cain would get it worked out.

Cain, the man who had just found out she'd had his child and hadn't told him. The man who still didn't trust her.

Panic crashed over her again.

"You know, some people just never readjust to life on the outside. Will do anything to get thrown back in," the same policeman who had put the cuffs on her said, his leer evident from the front seat. "Guess you must be one of those."

The reasonable part of her brain told her to just ignore him, but the terror wouldn't let her. "Please. This is some sort of mistake. I had authorization to take off the anklet."

"Is that so? You'd be amazed at how many people are 'authorized' to do whatever they want to, right up to the point where they get caught."

The handcuffs pulled at her shoulder blades, making sitting in the car uncomfortable and reminding her that she swore she would never be back in this position again. How long would they keep her? She needed to call Ariel and let her know what was going on. Did she need a lawyer? And where was the other officer who had his gun pointed at Cain? What was taking them so long?

Finally the other officer walked out the door with Cain behind him. Hayley's eyes devoured Cain's face, hoping to find a glimpse of good news, that he'd been able to convince these men of their official work.

"Ends up Agent Bennett is, in fact, federal law enforcement, and does have what looks like a legitimate court order for the removal of the tracking device," the nice cop—Hayley knew Cain had asked his name but she couldn't remember it—said.

Bad Cop just snickered. "Not my problem. They're going to have to fight it out downtown."

"I told him the same."

Hayley's eyes flew to Cain's again as he walked closer to the car.

"Hey, back off," Bad Cop said. "I don't care who you work for."

"Chill out, Brickman, for crying out loud," Good Cop muttered.

Cain ignored them both, his eyes on Hayley. "Six hours, okay? We'll have this worked out and you back home in six hours. Just hang on until then."

Hayley nodded. Everything in his green eyes told her she could trust him. He would handle this.

"Okay," she said softly. It was all she could do. Her life was in his hands now. She prayed trusting him wasn't the biggest mistake she'd ever made.

Chapter Eleven

Cain called Ren on the way to the courthouse.

"Cain, you know we're not dating, right? I talk to you more than I talk to some of my girlfriends."

Any other time Cain would've harassed Ren about his love life, but the look in Hayley's eyes as she had sat in that squad car had crushed all ability for humor in him.

"State troopers came and arrested Hayley a few minutes ago for violation of her parole, having to do with the anklet."

He heard Ren's muttered curse. "The court order was legit. What the hell happened?"

"That's what I'm trying to find out. Something's not right here, man."

"Damn straight. She's only had the thing off for what, thirty-six hours? That's pretty quick to pounce on a nonviolent parolee. Let me see what I can find out."

Cain could hear a keyboard clacking away. Ren's

curse was quite a bit more foul when it came a few minutes later.

"What?" Cain asked.

"You still got a hard copy of that court order?"

"Yes. Why?"

"Because our entire petition and agreement from the judge has been completely erased from the system."

"What the hell? How does that happen?"

"It doesn't, Cain. Not unless someone gets inside the system and deliberately erases it."

Now it was Cain's turn to curse. "Is it the Omega mole? Does he know we're onto him? Or Damien Freihof? He's been one step ahead of us this entire time."

"It will take a while to backtrack this and figure out who did it. Ironically your gal Hayley would be the best one to do that."

"Yeah, well, I don't think they're going to let me take my laptop into her cell." Cain gritted his teeth as he changed lanes to lead him into the parking lot of the criminal courthouse. "And I can't get the help I need from the Omega office without tipping off the mole."

"Let me see what I can find from here," Ren said.

Ren McClement worked out of Washington, not the Critical Response Division office in Colorado Springs. Hopefully the mole wouldn't have knowledge of Ren's activities.

"Okay. Meanwhile I'll use this paper copy of the

court order and see if it gets me anywhere." He told Hayley six hours. He wanted to make sure he kept that promise.

"There's something not right here, Cain. First the fire and now this? It might be Freihof or the mole, but they should have no knowledge of your activities whatsoever."

Cain parked his car. "So either the mole is much more powerful than we think…"

"Or we're dealing with someone else entirely."

"Someone from one of my other cases? Targeting Hayley?" That didn't make much sense.

"We'll just see what we find."

"I made her a promise to get her out," Cain said. "She's more than done her time for whatever crimes she committed in the past."

Hayley's pale face, brown eyes huge, haunted his every thought.

"I'll hurry."

Inside the courthouse things went from bad to worse.

The judge who had signed the initial court order had gone on a last-minute fishing vacation and couldn't be reached for confirmation. Nearly growling in frustration, Cain was told it would be late afternoon before he could get time in front of another judge.

He decided he would use his federal law enforcement status to see Hayley while she was held in the booking area. He could at least give her information and reassure her—and himself—that things were going to be all right.

But once he got to that section of the building, he found that Hayley had been taken to the court section, an arraignment already scheduled.

An arraignment before a judge this soon after her arrest? That was almost unheard of. Normally someone might spend an entire day or even two in a holding cell before the judge was able to hear the initial details of the case and formally charge the defendant.

It wasn't normal, but at least it wasn't bad. Hayley would've been allowed to call, or would've been given, a lawyer. She would've told the lawyer what had happened, and Cain would be able to back up her statement and provide the document.

Hopefully it would all go away from there. Lumped up as some sort of clerical error.

Cain didn't know why they hadn't called him, so immediately found the courtroom where the arraignment hearing was taking place.

Hayley sat at a table in front of the judge's bench with a lawyer. Good, maybe her attorney had found a copy of the court order allowing Hayley near a computer, and this would soon be over.

Evidently the judge had different ideas. It was like watching her sentencing four years ago all over again. Powerless to stop any of it.

"It has come to my attention that not only have you violated your parole, Ms. Green, but that you have connection to violent criminals that the court was not aware of when you were initially paroled."

"Your honor…" Hayley's attorney tried to interject, but the judge held his hand up to silence the woman.

"I'll admit I'm not certain of all the facts here, so there will be no actual ruling by me today. But I am ordering that Ms. Green be taken back into custody and will return to the Georgia Women's Correctional facility until another parole hearing can be scheduled with all the facts."

What in the hell? Cain walked into the courtroom farther, pulling out his badge as he went.

"Your honor, I'm Agent Cain Bennett, with federal law enforcement, and was the person who had requested Ms. Green's original parole conditions be released. I have the court order in hand and want to assure you that she did not break any conditions of her parole."

Cain saw Hayley's head spin around to him, but he kept his eyes on the judge.

"Be that as it may, Agent Bennett, I do not have all the information needed to make any sort of judgment right now. Ms. Green will return to custody, but I'm sure with your word and the court order this could be worked out in just a couple of weeks."

"Your honor—"

The judge brought his gavel down on his table. "That's my decision. Bailiff, take Ms. Green into custody and prepare her to return to the correctional facility."

Frustration clawed through Cain. He rushed over to the row of seats directly behind Hayley's table.

"Hayley, we're going to get this worked out."

"I have to go back to prison." Shock clouded her tone, her entire face devoid of color.

Unlike last time when her eyes had seemed so deadened at what the judge said, this time they were filled with terror.

Cain couldn't help it, he reached up and trailed his fingers down her cheek. Agony clawed at his gut. "I'm sorry, sweetheart. But I promise I'm not going to rest until I get this fixed. This is not like before. A couple of days. I promise you'll be back with me and Mason in a couple of days."

The bailiff reached Hayley and turned her around from Cain, placing handcuffs on her wrists in front of her.

Hayley glanced at him over her shoulder. "Take care of Mason." Her voice choked on the words.

"No, I won't need to. This will be less than a week and you'll be back."

Hayley didn't respond, just followed the bailiff, head down. Cain watched until she exited out the back.

He wanted to punch something, throw over the table in front of him, but knew that would just get him arrested, too. He needed to work the problem.

Cain spent the rest of the afternoon talking to

whoever he could to try to find answers. He phoned Ren to provide an update, but the call went straight to voice mail.

Ren would call as soon as he had any information.

Cain caught Hayley's attorney to ask her for details as she was leaving the courthouse. He walked with her.

"Ms. Rincon, I need to talk to you about Hayley Green."

She looked over at him dressed in a crisp tailored suit. This was no court-appointed attorney, this was someone who charged hundreds of dollars an hour for her legal services. Money Hayley didn't have, even if she'd known how to obtain the lawyer's services in such a short amount of time.

"Agent Bennett, I appreciate you speaking up for my client today in court, but I'm not allowed to talk about the case with anyone without my client's permission."

"I'm just trying to figure out what's going on. She was cleared by a judge to work with me and next thing we know she's been arrested for parole violation."

Rincon shrugged. "Look, I'll level with you. This shouldn't have been my case. I basically stood in today for a colleague in the public defender's department. This arraignment took place superfast and he needed help. So I got contacted at ten o'clock this morning and was asked to volunteer some of my time. I owed a favor so I did it."

Ten o'clock this morning? That would've been about the time the state troopers had arrived to arrest Hayley. How would a lawyer be called before Hayley was even at the courthouse?

"Ms. Rincon, there's something going on that's not right."

The woman shrugged. "I'll give you that it's all been pretty unusual, but I don't know that it's necessarily not right. But honestly, my part ends here. Someone else will be working with Hayley for her parole hearing. She can either hire her own lawyer or use a public defender."

This was a dead end. "Thanks for your time."

Rincon nodded and continued down the stairs from the courthouse.

An unknown lawyer asked to take Hayley's case before she was even arrested? An arraignment hearing in record time? Lost court orders and a judge suddenly on vacation?

Something definitely wasn't right.

Cain turned and went back into the building. He was about to cross some lines that might end up costing him his career, but he didn't care. His gut was telling him that Hayley was in danger and he damn well wasn't going to ignore that.

It took him an hour to find the circumstances he needed, as he waited for the assistant to Judge Nicolaides, who had held the arraignment hearing, to leave her desk.

Hoping this wouldn't cost him everything, but

willing to pay the price if it did, Cain slid inside the judge's inner chambers without permission.

The older man looked up from what he was reading, saw Cain and raised an eyebrow.

"You lost, son?"

"I need to talk to you, Your Honor."

"You are aware that you're not supposed to be in here, correct, Agent Bennett?"

Cain was surprised the judge remembered his name. "Yes, sir."

"I will give you five minutes. Only because I was there when you led the Spartans to the state championship."

Whatever the reason the judge was listening to him, even high school football, Cain would take it.

"I was telling the truth today about having the court order for Hayley Green to assist Omega Sector on a case."

"Then you'll want to be sure to share that information when they review her parole proceedings."

Cain gritted his teeth. He was afraid Hayley might not make it to the parole hearing. "Something's not right about this entire situation."

Judge Nicolaides leaned back in his seat. "Now see, normally I would hear something like that and think that it was based off of desperation and emotion rather than actual fact. But today, it just so happens, I might agree with you."

"Can you tell me why?"

"Ends up my early-afternoon hearings were

cleared off my schedule, and I was given just one. Ms. Green's case. I'm not one to complain about a lesser workload, but I must admit it did catch my attention."

"Hayley was arrested just this morning. About two hours before her hearing."

Judge Nicolaides's eyebrows seem to have found a new home in his hairline. "Two hours between arrest and her hearing? Again, normally I would say that Ms. Green had friends in high places to get before a judge that quickly."

"She doesn't."

"What also strikes me as peculiar about the situation is the fact that I was told that the case I would be hearing involved a criminal with, wait, let me find it"—the judge riffled through some papers and found the ones he wanted to read—"*significant potential for violence and destruction* if not returned to incarceration immediately, until more details could be produced to reevaluate her parole proceedings."

Cain could hardly keep himself from gawking. "Someone said that about Hayley Green? She was arrested for cybercrimes, has no violent history and did her time in a minimum-security prison."

"Son, you either don't know your friend very well, or someone very high up in the government has some pretty incorrect information. I'm sorry I don't have a name to give you."

"How high up?"

"Pretty damn high. Washington, DC."

"I don't understand."

"Neither do I. And I hope you can get this worked out when they reevaluate her parole. All I know is, today someone wanted to make sure your Hayley Green ended up back in prison."

Chapter Twelve

Cain couldn't go back home, not knowing that Hayley was sitting in a cell. He'd tried to see her, but had been told that she was being processed for relocation. Could not be seen until after she was transferred to Georgia Women's Correctional.

Was she scared? She would have to be. This had to be her worst nightmare.

He still hadn't heard back from Ren but knew the other man would get to him as soon as he had information. Meanwhile, Cain decided to do what he had promised Hayley. He would watch over Mason.

Cain parked his car outside Hayley and Ariel's small apartment complex with no intention of going inside. Not without Hayley, not until she was ready for him to meet Mason. That was the least he could do after everything that had happened. But he would keep watch over their building from here. He wasn't going to be getting any sleep anyway.

Tomorrow would involve finding the judge who was on vacation, the one who had given the initial court order for Hayley's assistance. Cain had no intention of waiting until she had an actual parole hearing to take in proof of the court order. He'd do it as early as possible.

She'd be transferred back to Georgia Women's Correctional tomorrow afternoon. At least once she was there Cain would be able to use his law enforcement credentials to see her.

It was not quite getting dark when the door of the apartment complex opened and Ariel and Mason walked out. They were holding each other's hands as they crossed to the small park half a block away. Cain got out of the car and followed them, careful to keep his distance.

Ariel sat on a bench while Mason ran around the wooden play area with a couple of other children. He ran full steam back and forth over a bridge, across monkey bars, and up and down slides. Cain couldn't help but be enthralled with him.

"You're going to make the other parents nervous if you keep standing there like a stalker," Ariel called out.

He crossed over to her but didn't sit on the bench beside her. "How did you know I was there?"

"I saw your car before we even left the apartment. Plus, Hayley gave me a heads-up that you might be around."

"Did she tell you what happened?"

"Briefly, in a very short phone call from her holding cell, not that she knew exactly what was going on. I resisted the urge to tell her that bad things happen to her whenever you're around. She's got enough to worry about."

"I'm going to get this fixed."

"You do that." Ariel didn't seem to have much more to say to him.

"She told me about Mason. That I'm his father."

"Being a sperm donor does not make you his father." Ariel's voice was tight.

"I plan to be his father in every way that Hayley will let me."

Ariel turned and glared at him. "You know, you're lucky that Hayley is a lot more forgiving than I am. Because I would've told you to go die in a hole."

Cain nodded curtly. "I get it, you're mad at me because I arrested her. And it sucked, I agree. But she did do it, Ariel, you know that, right? Hayley was guilty."

"Yeah, I know. But I also know that Hayley paid a much higher price than for any crime she'd actually committed."

Cain sighed. "Four years was a long time. I never dreamed she'd be sentenced for that long."

"You should've checked on her, Cain. What happened to her in that prison, nobody should have to bear that. Least of all someone like Hayley. Good. Gentle."

Cain wasn't sure what Ariel was talking about. He had checked up on her. Made sure she hadn't been hurt. There didn't tend to be many instances of violence in minimum security, but Ariel's words made him realize he must've missed something.

"What happened? Was she hurt?"

"Was she *hurt*? She gave birth in a prison hospital *handcuffed* to a bed. They didn't even let her hold Mason, did you know that? Not even one time."

"My God." He sank onto the bench next to her. He'd had no idea, hadn't even thought to ask her about the situation surrounding Mason's birth. Not that she would've told him if he had.

Ariel shook her head slowly. "It broke something in her. Not just that, but losing all that time in Mason's life."

"Believe me, if I could go back and change it, I would." Cain didn't know exactly what he would do, but everything would be different. "All I can do is try to make things right going forward."

"You're doing a fine job there, Ace, considering Hayley is back in jail."

"I'll make sure she's released. I'll make sure she's safe."

"Safe? Why do you say that? There's something else going on, isn't there?"

"Why do you say that?" he asked, throwing her words right back at her.

Ariel shrugged. "Something Hayley said the other day. About why she had to be working all the time. About why she had agreed to work for you, of all people."

"I was worried about her working so hard from the beginning. She shouldn't need money that badly."

Ariel kept her eyes on Mason. "Part of it is so she won't have to work so much once I leave to study in Oxford."

That made sense. "But you think there's something else?"

"I know there is. And believe it or not I actually told her to tell you, but I guess she didn't. She's been saving up money in case she has to run with Mason."

"Did she say why?"

Ariel shook her head. "No. She said the less I knew about it the better. But I know it has to do with her hacking stuff."

That didn't tell Cain anything concrete. It could be trouble that she might have to get away from, in which case he could help her. Or it might be trouble that she was running toward, and she wanted a safety net as she got out from underneath the law.

Cain looked over at the playground and saw that the kids seemed to be winding down. He stood up. "I'm going to go."

"Don't you want to meet Mason?"

He did. Wanted to hug him or shake his hand and ruffle his hair, whatever the kid felt comfortable with. He wanted to show him his own birthmark and how it was twins with what Mason had.

"Not without Hayley."

For the first time Ariel looked at him without utter

contempt schooling her features. "Then go get our girl, Bennett. She's lost enough time with her son, she shouldn't have to lose any more."

He stood up and walked away as Mason headed toward them.

"I'll bring her home."

BY THE NEXT morning Cain was convinced Ariel was right. From his laptop in the car outside Hayley's apartment, he'd spent the night researching the CET hacking scandal. There was something much deeper going on than what appeared on the surface.

Eleven people had been arrested along with Hayley four and a half years ago for their hacker work. The judge had made an example of the hackers, largely due to Senator Nelligar's involvement; although 90 percent of them had been first-time offenders, he had given them all, including Hayley, jail time.

They'd all been getting out of jail over the last few months.

Two of the twelve hackers had died in prison. One from injuries sustained in a fight, and another who had been thought to be mentally unstable the entire time and killed himself.

Things like that happened even in minimum-security prisons.

Three more had died in the last year since they'd been released from prison. Heart attack, car accident and drug overdose.

Five out of the twelve hackers arrested in the CET scandal were dead. That was way more than coincidence.

Coupled with what had happened to Hayley yesterday, Cain knew she was in trouble. *Life-and-death* trouble.

That was confirmed a couple hours later when he finally heard from Ren.

"I'm on my way to you right now," Ren said by way of greeting.

That wasn't good. If Ren wanted to be here, then things were even worse than Cain had thought.

"Then I guess you know we've got problems."

"Funny," Ren said. "I was about to say the same thing to you."

Cain told him about the deaths of so many of the hackers who had been arrested with Hayley.

"Add another heart attack to your list," Ren responded.

"One of the hackers? Did I miss something?"

"The judge from whom you got the original court order releasing Hayley?"

"The guy on the fishing vacation?"

"Yep," Ren said. "Heart attack."

Damn it. "So the one man who could've very quickly corroborated our story just died."

"Cain, it gets worse from there."

"Worse than six people being dead?"

"I was hitting dead ends in normal channels trying to figure out what was going on with Hayley," Ren continued. "So I took to unofficial channels."

Like everyone in Omega Sector, Cain wasn't sure exactly what Ren McClement's actual job description was. The man's name was mentioned with a sort of reverence. Rumors were that McClement's specialty was undercover ops. Deep, long-term assignments. The ones no one with family or friends could take because the infiltrated groups wouldn't hesitate to kill a loved one just to see what the person would do.

McClement answered to very few people and always got his man, no matter what the cost.

If Hayley was in as much trouble as Cain was afraid she was, he wanted someone like Ren at his back.

"What did you find out from unofficial channels?"

Ren let out a breath. "There's a hit out on Hayley's life."

Cain's curse was low and foul. "Who? Why?"

"That, I haven't been able to find out. But it's someone high, Cain, really high."

Cain thought of what Judge Nicolaides had said. Almost the exact same thing.

"When? How?" Those were the questions Cain should've been asking first anyway. The who and why could wait.

"Somebody is willing to pay top dollar to kill Hayley in what looks like an escape attempt as she's transferred to the correctional facility today."

Cain knotted his fist against his kitchen counter. "Okay, I'll get on the phone and stop the transfer.

Unless they've got a bus already going out there, they probably meant to transfer her in a squad car."

"That's just it. The channels I got this from contain some crooked cops. I'm not sure who we can trust."

"Then I'll go get her out of holding right now. We won't even let the transfer start." This time he wouldn't take no for an answer when it came to seeing her.

"You're not going to be able to get her out. Someone's already been changing the electronic files surrounding her. Instead of cybercrimes, Hayley's file now says that she was a violent criminal, brought in as a fugitive."

Cain was already bringing up the information on his laptop. Sure enough, after logging in to the Georgia law enforcement system, he saw everything Ren said was true. Instead of cybercrimes, she was listed as having done time for attempted murder and assault. She'd escaped from custody and had been on the run when she was caught.

There was no way the police would release Hayley to Cain.

"And even worse," Ren said, "they're not taking her back to the minimum-security prison. They're taking her to maximum security. If for some reason she lives through the transfer, whoever put out this hit has made it open season on Hayley once she arrives."

Chapter Thirteen

The hardest part about prison for Hayley had been the lack of privacy. Followed at a very close second by boredom.

Books had helped a great deal with the boredom since she hadn't been allowed near any computers while incarcerated. She'd read just about every title in the library. She'd used nonfiction books to learn about things directly related to her like child rearing, psychology, cooking and nutrition. She also learned about stuff not so related to her: climbing Mount Everest, cooking Thai food and the five-hour work-week. She'd read all sorts of fiction. Action, horror, science fiction. The only thing she hadn't been able to read was romance. Books with happily-ever-afters just didn't seem to apply to her at all.

She had no books now. And no privacy again. The county holding cell was like a twenty-four-hour diner, women coming in and out constantly. All night she'd been watching them, since sleep had been impossible.

When she had been in prison, she had pretty much been ignored. Nothing about her four years at the Georgia Women's Correctional facility had been traumatic. No one had hurt her, there hadn't been fights or people shanking others, or anything that might happen at a maximum-security prison that held the more violent offenders.

Minimum security hadn't even had barbed wire fences surrounding the facility. It had been sort of like camp, except you couldn't leave, and the counselors had guns. And they didn't really pay attention to you unless you did something bad.

None of the officers seemed to be ignoring her now. Every time one walked by, he or she glared at Hayley, anger clear in their expressions. She had no idea what she had done to warrant such hostility.

But she just kept thinking about the guards and the books and anything else except for the fact that in a couple hours they would be taking her back to prison. Maybe for a long time.

Because if she concentrated on that, the hysteria was going to bubble over. It was so close to the surface right now she could feel it.

She wanted her son. Wanted to be with Mason. He was just getting used to her being in his life and now she was gone again.

And Cain…so much of this was resting in his hands. And he had so much reason to hate her.

"Hayley Green?" An officer opened the cell door

and Hayley walked over. "You're being transferred to Georgia Women's Max."

The maximum security? "No, I think there's been a mistake. I'm supposed to be transferred, but it's to the minimum-security prison."

Hayley could hear the other women in the cell snicker.

The officer placed handcuffs around her wrists. "Look, I just get the people lined up for the transfer, I don't decide who goes where." He looked her over, evidently deciding maybe she didn't look like a violent criminal. "But I'll double-check your paperwork."

The panic ratcheted up another level. Maximum security? Hayley knew only what she had heard about it from other inmates.

And that was enough to know that people like her didn't last long.

She forced herself to deliberately breathe in and out, to try to keep the anxiety tamped down. The feel of handcuffs around her wrists didn't help. Amazing how two relatively small circles of metal could make someone feel so claustrophobic.

Hayley was stopped at a desk while the guard checked the paperwork.

"Sorry, kid." He was actually nice enough to hold the papers out for her to read herself.

Sure enough, it said that she was to be transferred to the maximum-security prison, about eighty miles south of here. It had been signed by a judge.

Breathe in. Breathe out. Hayley just focused on that as she was led outside. This time she wasn't going on a bus with other inmates, she was being transferred in a squad car.

"Look," the officer said as they arrived at the car, "just keep quiet when you get there. Don't demand anything in front of other prisoners. As soon as you can, ask to see your lawyer. Your lawyer can get this straightened out."

Hayley nodded, but could barely make sense of his words in her panicked state.

Breathe in. Breathe out.

That guard left and another voice rang out. "Well, well, well. Seems like I have the luck of being with you twice in two days."

It was Officer Brickman, who had arrested her yesterday.

"Looks like I'm your ride today."

Hayley didn't respond. The other, nicer officer who had been with Brickman yesterday didn't seem to be anywhere around. Another younger man walked up to the vehicle.

"I'm Jarod Abrams. I've been assigned to partner with you in escorting the prisoner."

Brickman didn't seem happy about that. "I let them know that I could handle the transfer by myself when my normal partner got reassigned today. Not like she's going to be a problem."

The younger man shrugged. "Just doing what I've

been ordered to do. And because I don't think they want any prisoners only escorted by one person."

Brickman's jaw tensed, but he didn't argue further. "Well, let's get on the road then." He climbed into the passenger side, leaving Abrams to drive.

Hayley withdrew into herself as they drove. The metal around her wrists seemed to rub no matter how she tried to move. Brickman and Jarod Abrams talked but she paid little attention. At one point they began arguing about a shortcut when Brickman demanded Abrams pull off the highway and onto a more isolated two-lane road leading toward the countryside. Abrams didn't seem to want to, but he did it.

She was staring out the window at nothing, wondering if she might completely lose it and start bawling at any moment, when she realized Officer Brickman was talking to her.

"Is that true, Green?"

Hayley tore her eyes from the window up to him. "Is what true?"

"That you have a knack for getting out of handcuffs? That's what I heard."

Hayley had no idea what he was talking about. She no more knew how to get out of handcuffs than she knew how to do a backflip.

She held up her arms, showing they were completely secure. "I guess you heard wrong."

Brickman chuckled. "It's still what I'm going to say."

Abrams looked over from where he was driving. "Say when?"

"When they ask me how Green got out of her cuffs and tried to escape."

Before Hayley could figure out what was happening, Brickman reached over and jerked the steering wheel out of Abrams's hands, causing the car to spin around and go partially off into the small ditch that paralleled the isolated road.

Hayley was jerked painfully to the side as the car stopped, slamming her against the door, unable to catch herself easily with her cuffed hands.

"What the hell, Brickman?" Abrams yelled.

Brickman pulled his gun out and pointed it at Abrams. "Get out of the car."

"What the hell is going on?"

Brickman shook his head. "I didn't want anybody else to get hurt and went to considerable trouble to get my regular partner reassigned. Not to mention he's a Goody Two-shoes, and would've never gone along with this."

"Gone along with what?" Abrams asked.

Brickman just kept his gun trained on the other man. "Out of the car."

Hayley tried to shrink down in the back seat. Whatever was happening, she didn't want to be part of it.

Sure enough, as soon as Abrams had gotten out of the car, Brickman shot him twice in the chest.

Hayley gasped as the younger man fell to the ground.

"Kid should've been wearing his vest. I guess this will teach him." Brickman turned back to Hayley, yanking the car door open. She expected him to shoot her right there, but instead he reached for her.

"Come on, you and I have got to stage a huge escape attempt. I'm going to get fired for this, you know." He grabbed her by the hair and yanked her out of the car. Hayley couldn't stop her cry of pain. "But the half a million I'm going to get for killing you will more than make up for it.

"I'll tell them I made Abrams stop so I could take a piss. That's what will actually get me fired—breaking the rules like that. Then the kid, being a soft heart, not knowing how dangerous you were, and your ability to get out of handcuffs, let you out of the car."

Hayley had no idea what Brickman was talking about.

He pulled her toward the top of the ditch. "You guys tussled. I came over to help. You shot him with my gun."

Hayley was still trying to wrap her mind around what he was saying and totally wasn't prepared for his fist that caught her on the jaw. She fell to the ground.

Brickman stood over her, sneering. "I'd love to have a little fun, but we're kind of in the open out here. So I guess I should just get on with the killing you part."

Hayley twisted so she was on her back. He had the gun out again, pointing it straight at her. Hayley had no idea what his whole monologue had been about, but damned if she was just going to lie here and let him shoot her.

Because one of the other books she'd read while in prison was about self-defense for women.

She swung her leg to the side and then brought it back toward him, hooking her ankle at his knees. He cursed as he fell to the side.

Hayley tried to scurry away, but Brickman grabbed her by the leg and pulled her back. A punch to the stomach doubled her over, stealing her breath.

"You know, you fighting me is just adding credence to my story."

Hayley swung out with her elbow and cracked him in the face, glad to see when blood started gushing out of his nose.

"Screw this." Brickman brought up his gun and Hayley knew this time it was really over.

Until a car rammed into the squad car parked just a few yards away from them.

Not sure what was happening but knowing it was her chance, Hayley scurried away. She heard Brickman's ugly curse but she didn't turn around, hoping he'd be so involved with whatever had happened at the car that she could make her escape.

But a flying tackle had her slamming back against the ground, air once again knocked out of her. Brickman spun her around until she was lying on top of him, her back to his chest, then stood, arm wrapped around her neck.

"Put the gun down or I'll kill her right now." Hayley could feel the muzzle of Brickman's gun against her head.

"It's over, Brickman. You're not going to see any of that money, so you might as well let her go."

Hayley almost sobbed with relief when she heard Cain's voice. She had no idea how he'd found them or even known she was in trouble and right now didn't care.

"We know about the contract on her, but that's not happening," Cain continued.

"I may not get the money, but I can still kill her." Brickman jerked his arm tighter around Hayley's throat. She brought up her still-cuffed hands to try to get some air.

Brickman just laughed. "You know what, Bennett? I wonder how many times I can bring her to the point of almost passing out from lack of oxygen while we stand here playing our little standoff game? That's pretty painful for her, don't you think?"

His words began to fade as black spots started overwhelming her vision. She could feel herself beginning to droop when all of a sudden the pressure released and she was able to suck in air again. She breathed the beautiful oxygen as deeply as she could.

Then before she could even fully recover, the oxygen was cut off again. She whimpered and began to struggle, desperately pulling at Brickman's arm, but couldn't get more air.

"Your choice," Brickman said from behind her.

"Fine," Cain said, his voice less calm. "Give her air. I'm putting the gun down."

After a moment, Brickman's hold loosened again. Hayley breathed, so thankful for air, but wanted to tell Cain not to put his gun down. Surely he had to know Brickman would just kill them both.

"See?" Brickman said. "That's the problem with all you federal agents. You think everyone's going to follow your rules."

Brickman moved the gun away from her temple to point it at Cain. Before she could even react, he was forcefully thrown away from her and then knocked unconscious onto the ground with a single punch from a man who'd crept up behind them.

He'd moved so silently Hayley hadn't even known he was anywhere around. The guy took another step forward and kicked the gun out of Brickman's unconscious fingers.

"Damn well took you long enough," Cain said, rushing to Hayley.

"Didn't want to take too much of a chance of this pretty lady's head getting blown off by that bastard's gun," the big man said. He tilted his own head toward hers. "Ma'am. Ren McClement."

Hayley nodded before finding herself wrapped in Cain's arms.

"Are you all right?" Cain asked, moving his hands gently over her face and shoulders, kissing her temple.

"He was going to kill me." Her voice sounded raspy even to her own ears.

"Hey, baby cop over here is still alive. We need to call an ambulance," Ren said.

"Hayley can't be here when the police arrive." Cain was still looking her over, making sure she didn't have any serious injuries. "They'll merely take her back into custody and she'll be in just as much trouble as she was."

"I'll stay here with them," Ren said. "Pull the good old Texas boy who wandered into trouble act. I'll say it was just the two men when I got here."

Cain nodded. "She and I will have to leave on foot. So stall them as long as possible."

Ren smiled. "You'd be amazed at how long it takes a Texan to tell a story sometimes."

"Good thing I know you're not from Texas." Cain reached down and grabbed the handcuff keys from Brickman's belt and unhooked Hayley's hands. He rubbed her wrists gently from where the metal had abused them. He took the cuffs and locked Brickman's hands behind his back, ignoring him as he moaned.

"We're going to have to run. Can you make it? Once we leave here you're going to be a fugitive. But until we figure out what's going on and how to stop it, that's safer than being in police custody."

"We have to get to Mason and Ariel. I think they're not safe, either."

Cain nodded. "I've already sent someone to pick them up."

"Who? Police? Can we trust them?" Hayley wasn't sure whom she could trust anymore.

"Actually, Brickman's partner, Perowne. We knew someone would be trying to kill you on the way to the prison, but it was him who tipped us off that Brickman used this shortcut, even though he'd been reprimanded about it before. If Perowne hadn't called me, I wouldn't have made it to you in time."

Hayley nodded, still trying to figure out exactly what was going on. She just wanted to get to her son.

"You guys better get out of here. Paramedics are on their way. I'm sure the locals won't be far behind." Ren was keeping pressure on Abrams's wounds.

They began walking across a field at a brisk pace, getting away from the road.

"Nearest town's about four miles. I can arrange a ride for us there."

She took in a deep breath through her sore throat. "Okay."

"And then you're going to tell me everything, Hayley. Every. Damn. Thing. What it is you know or have done that has someone trying to kill you. We're not going to have any more secrets between us."

Chapter Fourteen

Their escape didn't leave much time for talking. The trill of sirens filled their ears before they were more than a few minutes away, prompting them to move more quickly.

"Don't worry, Ren will buy us some time." But Cain urged her to increase her speed with a hand on the small of her back.

"Is he really not from Texas?"

"Boston, I think. But with Ren nobody knows for sure."

"But he's Omega Sector?"

"Yes. One of the best."

They picked up speed again and traveled in silence for a long while.

"Brickman was going to make half a million dollars to kill me," she finally said.

Cain glanced at her. "And do you know who was offering that money?"

She knew she was going to have to tell him everything; she just hoped she could prove it.

"I don't know the name of the person, but I think I have a way of finding out."

Cain nodded. "We'll talk about it more once we're not in the open."

Relief flooded her that he was at least willing to listen to what she had to say. Wasn't just automatically lumping her into the criminal category. Given all the secrets between them, that was the best she could hope for right now.

It didn't take long before keeping up with the slow jog pace Cain was setting became too much for her. Lack of sleep, lack of food, almost getting killed, were all taking their toll. She stumbled.

And he caught her arm and helped her right herself. "Let's slow down for just a minute."

Hayley shook her head. "No, it's all right. I know we've got to hurry."

But she could feel herself start to shake. Every time she swallowed she could feel where Brickman had choked her. When she moved she could feel where the cuffs had cut into her skin.

Cain put both hands on her shoulders, concern clear in his eyes. "Hayley…"

She couldn't fall apart right now, there was too much at stake, too far to go. But tears she couldn't control began streaming down her face.

"I'm sorry. This is stupid—"

She didn't get any other words out as she was yanked against Cain's chest, his arms surrounding her in a cocoon of safety.

"It's okay. God, Hayley, what you've been through. It's okay to cry."

He kept her against his chest as sobs erupted out of her. He murmured soft words about her strength and her spirit and how she wasn't alone in this anymore.

She could almost feel his strength seep into her. Cain could handle anything. Knowing he was on her side made everything seem more bearable.

"Better?" he asked.

She sighed. "Except for being a blubbering idiot."

He shook his head. "You shouldn't. I've seen trained agents crack under less pressure than you've been under. And crying for all of two and a half minutes doesn't count as cracking." He pulled her close to him again.

Hayley breathed in his scent. It hadn't changed much in all these years. Deep and musky and uniquely Cain. She hadn't thought she'd ever really experience it again.

"Ready to go?" he asked, without pulling away from her.

She nodded. "Let's go get our son."

A half an hour of brisk walking later they made it to the town.

"What do we do, call a cab?" Hayley asked.

Cain shook his head. "No. We're too far south of Gainesville and it will be the first thing the cops look for."

"Do you want me to call Ariel and have her come

get us?" Hayley didn't like the thought of bringing Ariel and Mason closer to the danger, but knew she and Cain had to get out of here.

"No. We're going to steal a car." Cain shrugged. "Since we're already fugitives and all."

He didn't look too worried about it, so she didn't press. He found an old truck parked near the back of the town's hardware store. After ripping out the small panel and crossing some wires, they were on their way.

She shook her head. "You know, considering I'm the ex-con, you sure do have some lawbreaking skills."

He grinned at her, that grin she hadn't seen since high school. The one that still melted her heart, and certain intimate clothing pieces. It was all she could do to not reach over and brush that errant dark curl off his forehead.

"Sometimes to help keep the peace you have to know how to break the law."

A line she never thought she'd ever hear from Mr. Black-and-White.

A call from Officer Perowne had them going to his apartment rather than Hayley's. Cain put it on speakerphone.

"I was here with them, like you asked, when a call came over the scanner," Perowne said. "A domestic dispute call, with a child involved."

"Let me guess, it was for Hayley and Ariel's address."

"Yep," Perowne replied. "I got Ariel and the boy

out quick, but almost wasn't fast enough. The squad car got there maybe twenty seconds after we made it to my car."

"Did you see who it was? Because that's probably somebody else on the killer's payroll."

"No. I just wanted to get them out of there."

Hayley's hands clenched into fists in her lap. She couldn't stand to have the danger so close to Mason. Cain talked a little bit more with Perowne, got his address and hung up.

"Were they going to kill them?" Hayley asked. "Do you think that's what the people who went to the apartment were sent to do?"

"I doubt it. It wouldn't help anyone's cause to kill Mason and Ariel outright. Domestic dispute sounded like it was a setup to be able to take Mason into custody."

"To get me back into their hands."

Cain nodded. "If I had to guess, yes. You know something or can do something that someone very powerful wants eliminated."

Hayley nodded. "It has to do with the CET case."

"I figured as much."

"Why?"

"Because of the twelve of you who were arrested, five are dead. None of the deaths individually are suspicious, but when you look at them as a whole…"

Hayley felt like the air had been sucked out of her lungs. "Someone's hunting the people involved in the case."

Cain glanced at her before turning his eyes back to the road. "Yes. And if I had to make a guess, it's because they don't know which one of you has the damaging information. But I'm assuming it's you."

She didn't know if he was going to believe her. Heck, she was the one who had discovered what was going on and still found it hard to believe.

"I know I told you the other night that about a month before I was arrested I had decided to get out of the hacking scheme."

Cain nodded, but she was at least glad to see his jaw didn't tighten the way it had all the other times they had talked about her arrest.

"I wasn't stupid," she continued. "I didn't want to go to jail, so I was going back into the CET system to cover my tracks."

She turned and looked out the window.

"Vargas was the one who banded the hackers together. I didn't know about any of the others and they didn't know me. Basically he had the contacts to sell our results. All of us individually could've hacked the system, but we wouldn't have known how to make money with what we had found."

"So he was the auctioneer. The middleman connecting the buyers with the sellers."

"Yes. The CET was pretty complicated to hack, even for us. The test is different at every testing center, and we had to crack that algorithm in order to know what set of questions would be present at any particular testing session."

"That's why CET called itself unhackable."

Hayley shrugged. "It probably is as a whole. But we weren't trying to hack it as a whole."

The CET was so popular because students could get their results immediately instead of having to wait weeks like previous college testing required. But in order to get the results so quickly, the test had to be computerized.

Anyone who said something couldn't be hacked was a liar. If it was on any sort of open system, it could be hacked.

"Okay," Cain said. "This all came out in the trial. Doesn't seem like anything out of the ordinary."

"It's not. It's when I dug much deeper to try to hide my tracks that I discovered the real problem."

"Tell me."

"Most of the CET exams are at high schools all over the country. That's where we concentrated almost all of our hacking. But there are American high schools on foreign soil at US military bases across the world. The CET system also does testing there. For both American and foreign kids."

"Okay, that seems right."

"I found out someone was using the tests to send information that had nothing to do with the exams themselves."

He glanced at her again. "What sort of information?"

She swallowed. This was where he either believed her or called her crazy. "State secrets, Cain. To be honest, some of it I didn't even understand. But in one transmission it was definitely weapon plans."

Cain's curse was low and foul. "Someone is using the CET for espionage."

Hayley let out a breath she hadn't even been aware she was holding. "Yes. I don't know how deep it goes. I was just starting to dig into it when I was arrested."

"So whoever is behind it knew someone had discovered something, but didn't know who. And is probably the one who put law enforcement on the hackers' trail to begin with."

It made sense. "They needed to flush the hackers out. And once we'd been arrested—"

"All they needed was to pick you off one by one," Cain finished for her. "Until they either found the person who knew, or had eliminated you all."

He believed her. Something inside her eased. She couldn't offer any proof yet, but he still believed her.

"I put in an electronic trapdoor before I was arrested. Once I can get back online freely I can access that. It will point me in the direction of who's behind the secret selling."

"Will it expose you?"

Hayley nodded. "Yes. Whoever it is will definitely know it's me who accessed the information."

"Then it's a race to see if you can get the information into the right hands before they find you." His hands tightened on the steering wheel. "That's why you were saving up money to run."

She nodded with a shrug. "I thought I had at least

two years before I could access a computer and that would make me safe."

"But working for me gave you access early and whoever is behind this obviously has some law enforcement in their pocket."

She brought a hand up to her sore cheek where Brickman had hit her. "I don't know how high up this goes, but it has to be pretty high. They're going to be looking for me, right? So what do we do?"

"For now, we run."

Chapter Fifteen

Hayley's story explained a lot, and Cain had no reason not to believe her, especially after the contract out on her life. Ren had dealt with the situation with Brickman—he'd be going to jail, especially since the officer he'd shot had miraculously survived and would be testifying against him. But that didn't mean there wouldn't be someone else after Hayley soon.

It was time to kill two birds with one stone.

He was taking Hayley where he could protect her and she could get the information he needed about the Omega mole: inside the Critical Response Division headquarters in Colorado Springs.

Cain had already talked to Steve. Hayley would be working in a section of the building far from active agents, and therefore away from the mole. It would give her a chance to dig deeper into both the CET situation and the Omega traitor. Now he just needed to get them to Colorado. Flying wasn't an option, so they would be driving.

They hadn't gone to her apartment after picking

up Ariel and Mason; it was too risky. Until everything was cleared up, Hayley was a fugitive to all law enforcement, and a huge potential paycheck for the compromised ones.

So, as they'd explained to little Mason, they were going on a road trip.

He'd met his son. Cain still could barely believe it. Mason had been excited to see "Mama Hayley" when they'd arrived, rushing into her arms. She'd held him to her, hands stroking over his little head, before letting the little wiggle-worm go. Ariel and Hayley had embraced—Ariel still giving Cain the evil eye—while Cain had explained the situation as best he could to Officer Perowne, thanking him for his help.

Then Cain had crouched down and met his son, his green eyes—a replica of his own—staring back at him.

"Mason, this is Cain." She hadn't tried to offer any more details. Mason was too young to understand family dynamics anyway.

Mason looked from Hayley to Cain. "Like candy cane?"

Cain hadn't been able to stop his big grin. "Sure, buddy. You can call me Candy Cain."

He'd held out his hand, unsure of what exactly he expected the little boy to do. Shake it?

Mason had slapped him five, smiled and run off, muttering about Candy Cain and road trips.

Cain couldn't stop looking at Mason in the rearview mirror now that they were on their way. Hayley was in the back seat of the car he'd rented, playing a color game with Mason. She'd also read him books, sung songs and played peekaboo.

"She loves him more than anything," Ariel muttered from the seat beside Cain when Hayley and Mason broke into another rendition of "The Wheels on the Bus." "She's an excellent mother. You better not do anything to take Mason away from her."

Cain looked over at the other woman, honestly shocked. "I would never do that. Especially not now. Not seeing how much she loves him. I want to protect them both."

"Good. Because Hayley deserves that. Deserves to have time with her son as just a mom. Deserves to have someone in her life who isn't going to always lord over her the fact that she once made a mistake—"

"Ariel," Hayley said from the back seat. Cain realized the singing had stopped. Mason had fallen asleep. "That's enough."

"Why? Someone needs to say something to him."

This time it was Hayley he saw when he looked in the rearview mirror. But she was staring at the back of Ariel's head.

"Cain isn't the villain here."

"Yeah, well, I'm not sure he's the hero, either," Ariel snapped back.

"We both made mistakes in the past," Cain said. "Both have things we would take back if we could."

Now Hayley's eyes met his. She nodded. "But

right now the most important thing is looking forward. There's too much at stake to bicker about the past."

She looked back at Mason.

But what Ariel said had been right. If Cain ever truly wanted to be a part of Hayley's life, he was going to have to let go of the hacking. Accept, like he'd said, that they'd both made mistakes. Not lord hers over her.

But Hayley was even more right. If they couldn't work out the problems of their present, the ones of the past weren't going to matter.

They drove as long as they could while Mason was asleep, knowing they'd have to stop and let him get some energy out once he woke up. Cain's call to Ren assured him that things seemed quiet, or that there was at least no direct word out in what direction they were heading.

Cain got to know his son. When Hayley had offered to drive so Cain could sit in the back seat, he'd refused at first, afraid it would be awkward. That he would scare the boy or make him uncomfortable. But after a little encouragement—and providing him with a secret weapon, a small toy fire truck that was sure to enthrall Mason—Cain agreed. He soon discovered that his son loved fire trucks, but like all toy vehicles he played with, he liked to pretend they were roller coasters.

Both women in the front seat groaned when Mason began to make a strange noise, bringing the fire truck up as far as his little arm, restrained in the car seat, would go. Then made a soft screaming sound as he brought it back down again quickly.

"He loves roller coasters," Ariel explained. "He's never been on one, but we've watched videos. So no matter what vehicle you give him to play with, he's going to pretty much act like it's a roller coaster."

Cain laughed. He and his brother had driven his parents crazy wanting to go to theme parks all the time as kids. "He comes by it honestly."

Cain played with Mason—seriously, the kid *really* loved to pretend his cars were on thrill rides—for hours, promising to take him to ride a roller coaster as soon as he was big enough. Cain's parents would love it, being dragged back out to a theme park once again, this time for their grandson.

He couldn't wait for them to meet Mason. Cain had been around him for only twenty-four hours and was already in love with him.

They drove through the night, taking turns. But by the second night, about eight hours outside of Colorado Springs, they decided to stop. Everyone needed to be out of the car, get a good night's rest in a bed.

Cain lent Ariel his burner phone for her to call and check her voice mail, since both women had ditched their cell phones so they couldn't be tracked. Cain offered the phone to Hayley, too, but she said no one would be calling her.

But she was wrong.

"Hayley," Ariel said after listening to her messages. "Some really Southern-sounding lady named Mara left you a message. Said she couldn't reach you on your phone and was worried maybe you were more hurt from the fire than you'd let on. Also says she has another job possibility for you both and to call her ASAP."

They watched as Ariel listened to what must've been another five or six messages from Mara, each obviously longer than the last.

"Let me just call her, okay?" Hayley finally said. "If not, she'll just keep calling. She was always looking after me at the Bluewater. I feel bad that she's so worried."

Cain nodded. "But don't give any specifics where we are. Just tell her you'll call her when you get back."

Although he had no plans to sit by and let her slave in some dead-end job where she had to work twelve hours a day washing dishes and mopping floors. He had contacts. People who would give Hayley a chance, just because he would vouch for her. Despite her past.

And he realized that was true. He would vouch for Hayley.

He heard her talking to Mara, remembered the older woman from the night of the fire.

"I'll definitely get in touch soon about the job, Mara. I've just got a couple of things to take care of." Hayley laughed. "No, I haven't been breaking my neck looking at all the papers, I promise. But thank you for checking on me."

He could hear Mara's drawl on the other end of the line but couldn't tell what she was saying.

"Thanks, Mara. I'll talk to you soon. Bye."

"Sounds like I've got a job at the local Waffle Hut if I want it," she said ruefully as she handed the phone back to Cain.

Over his dead body. "Let's finish this first, then worry about jobs."

Hayley nodded. Cain checked them into a hotel as Hayley got Mason's sleeping body out of the car. Cain had chosen a small town, well off the interstate, on purpose. The town had one main road with all the brick buildings, each two or three stories high, butting up to one another.

In a small town like this where the crime rate was low, credit cards and IDs weren't required for check-in. Cain paid with cash for two adjoining rooms, then parked the car a little way down the street, vehicle easily accessible from multiple directions. He didn't expect any trouble, but he wouldn't rest easily until they made it to the Omega Critical Response Division HQ.

Mason woke up as they got into the rooms, his internal clock off track due to their traveling. It was close to midnight, but he was wide-awake. Cain, Ariel and Hayley took turns playing with the little boy while the others showered.

"That's no fair," Cain said as Hayley sat on the

floor in front of Mason and the little boy brushed her long blond hair with a hairbrush.

Hayley laughed. "You say that until he turns the hairbrush backward accidentally and smacks my head with it."

Mason ran over to the bed where Cain sat, climbed up and started brushing his hair.

Hayley was right—it wasn't nearly as soothing as it looked.

She laughed again at the expression on his face. "Told you."

Cain would suffer all sorts of hairbrush torture to hear that laugh from Hayley. It relaxed Mason, too. He jumped down from the bed and ran back to Hayley. She distracted him this time with snacks.

Cain joined them on the floor and he and Mason pretended each cracker went over a roller coaster hill before ending up in their mouths.

Once the little boy had his belly full, he settled down, a big yawn taking over his entire face. Hayley brushed his teeth and put him in jammies, then brought him over to the bed.

"I'll just sleep in the other room," Ariel said, fresh from the shower. "You guys can stay in here."

Hayley looked concerned. "Are you sure?"

It was a balancing act between the two women, Cain knew. Ariel had been the mother figure to Mason for so long. Hayley didn't want to hurt her cousin in any way or remove her from Mason's life.

Ariel knew that, too. She rushed over to give Hayley a hug and Mason a kiss. She didn't even glare at Cain, so he considered that a win.

Mason's eyes were already drooping.

"Let's get him into bed before he falls asleep all over you." Cain pulled the bedding back so Hayley could lay Mason down from resting in her arms.

She crawled into bed next to Mason. "I'm just going to sleep here with him."

She wrapped her arm protectively around her precious son.

Cain walked over to turn off the light, leaving the bathroom light and fan on and the door cracked. He slipped off his shoes and got into the other bed. "I'll be right here."

There was no place else on earth he'd rather be.

Chapter Sixteen

Cain's eyes flew open and he held himself motion-less in the bed. Something had woken him up. What was it?

He could hear the even breathing of Hayley and Mason in the bed beside his. Was it Mason's occasional restless shifting on the bed that had woken him?

Something had him on high alert. After just a few moments he realized it was the silence that had caught his subconscious attention. The fan had cut off in the bathroom as well as the light. He looked over at the clock and it was also out. The power was out.

Cain silently shifted his weight from the bed, getting up and looking into Ariel's room. Power was out there, too.

It did happen. Hotels lost power. But he wasn't going to make the mistake of thinking it was a fluke. Not with everything that had happened in the last two days.

Cain silently stepped over to their second-floor window, keeping his body far to the side. He peeked out the farthest corner, careful not to shift the curtains.

The street outside was empty, no movement, as to be expected in the middle of the night. He allowed his vision to adjust even further. And then saw it.

A white van, halfway down the block, someone watching the building with binoculars in the driver's seat.

Cain forced himself not to make any sudden movements from the window, just gently stepped back.

They needed to get out of there.

Cain moved over to Hayley and put his lips close to her ear.

"Hays, wake up," he said softly, not wanting to wake up Mason.

Her eyes flew open. "Cain?"

"Yeah. We're in trouble. Somebody's cut the power to the building and there are people outside."

Cain had no idea how many or how rapidly and violently they would be approaching.

Hayley slid her arm out from under Mason and turned toward Cain, sitting up.

"What do we do?"

"Get your shoes on and wake up Ariel. We've got to get out of here."

Hayley nodded and got up, padding softly into the other room.

Weapon drawn, Cain stuck his head out the door and looked up and down the hall. No one was out there, which was a good sign. Whoever was after them wasn't going to come in guns blazing, or they'd already be here.

He shut the door and turned and faced Ariel and Hayley, concern evident in both their faces.

"Is there anyone out there?" Ariel asked.

"Not yet. My bet is that they have the front and rear exits guarded, and plan to pull the fire alarm and take us as we rush out."

Hayley's face lost all color. "I can't let them take Mason. I'd rather give myself up."

Cain walked to her and cupped her cheeks with his hands. "It's not going to come to that."

Her hands came up and clutched his wrists. "Promise me we get Ariel and Mason out, if it comes down to it."

Cain nodded. He understood her fear and would make sure Mason was safe. But he had no intention of losing Hayley while doing that.

He dropped his hands and moved over to the window, careful once again not to disturb the curtains.

Definitely more action outside. Whoever was after Hayley could just use her fugitive status to incorporate local law enforcement into the chase. Cain didn't know if the people about to make their move were cops just doing their job or killers who didn't care who they hurt.

Then Cain saw a uniformed police officer walk up to the white van and tap on the window.

The man on the inside rolled down the window,

then, without warning, pulled out a gun with a silencer and shot the officer, point-blank.

Cain cursed under his breath. Guess that answered his question about who they were dealing with.

"Let's go. We've got to get out *right now.*"

"What happened?" Hayley asked as she slipped shoes on Mason's feet, the kid never even waking up.

He turned and looked at her. "Looks like it's some of Brickman's associates. They're going to shoot first, collect the reward later."

Hayley swept Mason's sleeping form up into her arms. "Let's go."

Cain checked the hallway once again and then led them out.

"If they're blocking both doors how are we going to get past them downstairs?" Ariel asked.

"We're not going down."

He hadn't chosen this hotel just because it didn't require credit cards. It had also been the best option in terms of multiple exit routes.

He led them to the stairs and cracked open a door. He signaled for the women to be as quiet as possible, and prayed Mason would stay asleep, as they began to climb the two stories up to the roof. He could hear the effort it was taking Hayley to carry Mason's dead weight, but couldn't afford to stop and offer to help. If Mason woke up and started crying it would all be over. After two flights they reached a small metal ladder.

"You okay?" he whispered to Hayley.

She nodded, shifting Mason slightly in her arms.

Cain climbed the five steps on the ladder leading up to the hatch going to the roof. The hatch door itself was old and rusted; he would have no problem getting it open, but there was no way he was going to do it quietly.

The next second the fire alarm began blaring. Cain didn't waste any time—noise didn't matter now. He used his shoulder to drive into the rusted hinges of the door, ignoring the pain as he felt it give way.

Ariel let Hayley up first since Mason had started crying with all the noise. She was struggling to get him up the rungs since he was now shifting his weight and trying to cover his ears. If she wasn't careful the boy was going to cause both of them to fall.

Cain reached down and grabbed Hayley under her armpits, hoisting both her and Mason up and onto the roof.

"Thank you," she muttered. Ariel climbed up right behind them and Cain put the door back in place.

"Where do we go now?" Hayley asked.

She wasn't going to like it. Hell, he didn't even like it.

He led them over to the east side of the building that was connected to the next one. They ran together onto the roof of the third building. Cain was thankful for the older design of the town, which caused the stores and shops to be built connected together to save money.

The next building had an outdoor fire escape.

They could use it to get down, but they would need to jump the five-foot gap between the buildings.

He saw Hayley's face as she realized what was going to happen. She began shaking her head.

Cain crossed to her. "We have to hurry. It won't take them long to figure out we are not in our room and the only way we could've gone was up."

"I can't make it with him," she said, features pinched.

"I can."

She nodded. Cain turned to Mason. "Hey, buddy. Want to play a game?"

The youngster looked skeptical. Cain couldn't blame him. "You and I are going to pretend to go on a roller coaster ride. Sound fun?"

Mason's eyes lit up and his little arms reached for Cain. Cain took his son for the first time and held him in his arms.

He just wished it wasn't because someone might burst onto the roof at any moment and try to kill them all.

"I'll go first in case you need help." Ariel backed up and ran, clearing the gap easily. She motioned for Cain to jump with Mason.

He felt Hayley's hand on his arm. He reached his hand under her nape and pulled her in for a quick kiss. "We'll make it."

Mason giggled. "You kissed Mama Hayley."

"Hang on, buddy," he whispered in the little boy's ear. "Time for our roller coaster ride."

Keeping one arm firmly planted around Mason's tiny middle, Cain pushed into a run, gathering more speed than he needed, just in case. A few moments later he was airborne, Mason's giggles in his ears.

Cain's feet hit the roof of the other building without any problem. He squeezed Mason quickly, then handed him to Ariel, who began leading him to the fire escape. "Be as quiet as possible."

Ariel nodded and Cain turned back to Hayley, who was already backing up to run.

The hatch door to the roof opened behind her, but it was too late to signal—she was already running. Cain pulled his firearm at the same time the man made it through and drew his own gun. The man shot at Cain first, causing Cain to dive to the side. He got off two rounds as he flew, killing the man.

But the man also got off a shot. At Hayley.

He heard Hayley's cry as the bullet hit her just as she left the safety of the roof. Instead of a smooth jump across like he and Ariel had, Hayley's body jerked, throwing her weight to the side.

She wasn't going to clear the ledge.

Her chest hit the corner and fingers pressed for a grip as she slid toward the edge. In his periphery, he could see Ariel pick up Mason and keep his head averted.

Cain dived for the ledge, grunting at the hard impact, his fingers grasping Hayley's just as she was falling.

"Got you." There was no way he was letting go.

She used her other hand to reach up and grab his wrist, even though he could tell it was painful for her.

"I'm okay."

Cain pulled her up and wrapped one arm around her, easing her to the ground.

"Where are you hit?"

"My side."

He lifted up her shirt and immediately saw the wound. It hit the fleshy part of the very outer edge of her waist, through and through. In terms of a torso shot, that was almost the best spot someone could hope for. It was bleeding, but obviously hadn't hit any critical organs.

"I know it has to hurt, baby, but we've got to get off this rooftop. As soon as the guy who shot you doesn't check in, they're going to know where we are."

Hayley nodded. "I can make it."

Keeping as much pressure on her wound as he could, he helped her off the ground and led her quickly over to the fire escape. Ariel continued her downward path with Mason.

"Do you want me to carry you?" He'd have to do a fireman's carry, which would probably be more painful for her, but the narrow stairs of the fire escape wouldn't allow him to carry her in his arms.

"No, I'll be all right."

He kept his arm around her as they made their way quickly down to the ground. Hayley made it, true to her word.

They kept to the shadows as they hurried down

the block to the car. Fortunately all the chaos at the hotel meant no one's attention was on them.

"You ride in the back with little man," Cain said to Ariel. Blood was already soaking through Hayley's shirt. Cain didn't want to scare him.

Ariel nodded and got Mason into his car seat while Cain got Hayley in the passenger seat.

"We need to get you to a hospital."

Hayley shook her head. "No. Once they realize one of us was wounded, they will be checking the hospitals. We can't take the chance."

The wound wasn't life-threatening, but that didn't mean it didn't hurt like hell. Hayley was sweating, her face pale.

"I can make it, Cain."

"You keep saying that."

He gritted his teeth, biting off a curse. They had to get out of here before they were noticed. Ariel passed up a clean T-shirt from the back seat and Cain gave it to Hayley.

"Keep pressure on your wound."

She nodded and he jogged around to the driver's side.

He started the car without turning on the lights, and drove down the side street. He didn't turn on the headlights until they were a mile outside of town. Soon they were speeding back toward the highway.

"What are we going to do?" Ariel asked, her hand reaching up from the back seat to wipe Hayley's sweat-soaked hair away from her brow.

"Do they have some sort of medical facility at

Omega headquarters?" Hayley asked. "Enough to patch me up?"

Cain looked over at her. Pain bracketed her mouth, but she didn't look like she was in danger of going into shock.

"Yes, we have excellent field medics." And it would be safe. "But we're six hours from Colorado Springs, and that's if I drive like hell."

Hayley's brown eyes pinned him. "Then drive like hell."

Chapter Seventeen

Hayley felt like her whole body ached. They'd been in the car for three hours, and she tried to console herself with the fact that they were more than halfway.

They'd stopped two hours ago at an all-night drugstore where Cain had bought hydrogen peroxide and gauze.

That had hurt.

But Cain had some basic medical training and he hadn't insisted on a hospital after seeing her wound more clearly. If it was that bad he would've insisted on a hospital despite the possible danger.

She grimaced as she shifted.

"How are you holding up?" He didn't glance over at her; he was going too fast to take his eyes from the road.

"How come people on TV and in movies who get shot jump up and run a marathon or something while looking gorgeous?"

"Because those people have stuntmen. They don't even *pretend* to get shot."

"I think I want to hire a stuntman for my next adventure."

She shifted to try to get more comfortable. But she couldn't. Physically or mentally.

The people chasing her had found them. Had found them and shot at them.

What if the man who had shot her had shown up fifteen seconds earlier? What if he had burst out when Cain had been jumping with Mason in his arms?

Hayley would've had no way to stop him. Cain and Mason would have plummeted to their deaths.

Hayley's heart turned icy at the thought.

Moreover, a truth had become clear to her.

She turned to Cain. "I can't run. I have to fight."

Cain gave a half shrug. "It's hard to fight when you don't know who your enemy is."

"My plan had been to buy myself some time. To stay off computers until I had enough money to run if I needed to. But that won't work. Look at how fast they found us."

"You're never going to have enough money to run from someone with this much power. Whoever found us this quickly is highly connected."

Hayley nodded. That much she already knew.

"What I said in the hotel is the truth to me." She glanced over her shoulder to where both Mason and Ariel were sleeping in the back seat. "Mason's safety is the most important thing. Ariel's, too. They are both innocent in all this."

"You're not guilty of these crimes, either, Hayley."

"I know. But it was my mistakes that led me down this path to begin with. I need to get Mason and Ariel somewhere safe so that I can figure out what to do."

"So *we* can figure out what to do. You're not alone anymore."

Hayley wasn't going to let Cain risk his life for this.

This was her fault and her fight. But she needed him. Needed his help.

Wanted to rely on the strength he offered. And once she figured out who was behind this, and how to catch them, then she would hand it over to him, let him do what he did best. Enforce the law.

But she wouldn't let him take a bullet for her, literally or figuratively.

The weight of it all bore down on her. She stared out the window wondering how the straight-A student she'd been in high school had become a fugitive ex-con with a bullet wound.

She felt his hand reach out and touch just above her knee. "Hey, did you hear me? You're not in this alone. I mean it."

His fingers left her leg and moved up to her cheek, making a gentle trail. Hayley couldn't help it; she leaned into his touch.

"All right," she said softly.

"I know a place where Mason and Ariel can stay and be safe. A friend from Omega Sector."

"How can you be sure this friend isn't the traitor we're searching for?"

Hayley didn't want to insult the bond of friend-ship, but she couldn't take a chance with Mason's life.

"Because the traitor and his partner, Damien Frei-hof, nearly killed my friend and his fiancée a few months ago."

That seemed like proof enough indeed.

"Ashton and Summer have a daughter, around Mason's age, so their house will be ready for kids and he'll have toys and stuff."

"Do you think they'll mind?"

"I think they are both willing to do anything, par-ticularly something as easy as opening their home to Ariel and Mason, to help bring these criminals to justice."

She couldn't help but smile. "Bring criminals to justice," she repeated in a deep voice, obviously mocking him. "I feel like you should be wearing a cape or something."

"I've got my cape in my closet at home. Maybe if you're good I'll let you see it."

It had been so long since she'd flirted she couldn't even remember how. She tried to think of something clever to say, but just smiled instead.

His hand reached over and squeezed her leg once more before returning to the steering wheel. She could swear she felt heat through her clothes where his fingers had been.

"Rest now," he said gently. "Capes and catching criminals in a few hours."

Hayley turned and looked back out the window. Sleep was a long time in coming.

"WHAT SHE CAN do is pretty amazing," Steve Drackett, head of the Omega Sector Critical Response Division, said to Cain thirty-six hours later. "And after a bullet wound? Even more incredible."

They were in a small set of rooms, not much bigger than closets really, in the corner of the headquarters building. This area, used for data entry and analysis, got neither much traffic nor much scrutiny from regular agents. The people in this section of the building definitely did not have the clearance, or inside information, to be the mole.

Steve had set them up with the computer resources Hayley needed to do both the tasks she was currently concentrating on. She had two full computers in front of her, each with its own keyboard. One system had two screens she could toggle between. Her fingers flew over the keys faster than Cain could even tap his on a table.

This was Hayley in her element.

"She's definitely impressive. And motivated."

They were watching her through a window, which allowed her to work without being distracted but also allowed Cain to be able to see what she was working on.

He hadn't asked for Steve to set them up like this, but he had to admit it made him feel a little better. Did he still not trust her completely?

"Someone coming after their young will cause even the most nonaggressive animals to fight. So I don't blame her for being motivated," Steve said. "And, by the way, congratulations. I hear you are a dad."

Cain knew the information would get around Omega as soon as Ashton and Summer saw Mason, when Cain and Hayley dropped him and Ariel off at their house. And of course Cain hadn't denied the truth when they had asked if the boy was his son.

"Yeah," Cain said to Steve. "Pretty big surprise."

Steve chuckled. "I can only imagine. Hell, I was shocked when Rosalyn showed back up in my life six months pregnant. Surprise child has to be a lot more jarring than surprise pregnancy."

"It caught me off guard, that's for sure."

"But she's a good mother?"

No matter what mistakes Hayley might've made in her past there could be no misinterpreting how much she loved Mason. "I couldn't ask for anything more for the mother of my child. She loves him completely and unconditionally."

Steve slapped him on the shoulder. "I'm glad to hear that. And I hope you won't make some of the same mistakes I did with my Rosalyn."

"And what would those be? I doubt you could have made as many mistakes as I have."

"I know that after Rosalyn hurt me once—well, didn't hurt *me*, hurt my *pride*—it was hard for me to let it go. I kept refusing to think she changed. Almost lost her because of it."

Cain watched Hayley. He wasn't studying the screens to make sure she was doing what she was supposed to, he was studying her.

"I trust her."

"Good. That's definitely important." Steve took a step back. "You'll let me know anything you find?"

"First thing. But I'll want to do it face-to-face. I don't trust any communication device in this building."

Steve nodded. "I agree."

As Steve opened the door he turned back. "Can an old man give you a word of personal advice?"

Now it was Cain's turn to chuckle. "You have a three-month-old at home and a gorgeous wife in her twenties. Plus, I don't think forty-one counts as old."

"Fair enough."

"But I'll still take your advice, especially if it has anything to do with this case."

"No, it has to do with your Hayley."

Cain just raised an eyebrow. *His* Hayley?

"I'm glad you guys worked out your trust issues. That you don't feel like you have to look over her shoulder all the time." Steve pointed in Hayley's direction. "But that woman in there needs more than just trust. She needs someone to care for her."

"I do care about her. Hell, I've cared about her since she was fifteen years old."

"Right now she needs the sort of care that shows action. She knows you'll fight beside her, particularly against anyone who will harm your child. But I think she needs to know that you're willing to fight *for* her, even if it's against her own inclinations and fears."

Steve didn't explain any further, just nodded and left.

Cain watched Hayley for a long time after the other man departed. Her hands continued to fly over the keyboards, one screen sorting through code like something out of *The Matrix*, another screen cross-referencing communication channels at Omega Sector. Every once in a while she would slide one section of code onto the other screen.

She shifted in her chair, stretching out her side. He knew it had to hurt. Even though the medic had agreed that no major damage had been done by her bullet wound and stitched the openings at the edge of her waist, it still had to be causing her great pain.

But here she was thirty-six hours later working, having only slept for about six hours the entire time.

She leaned closer to one of the screens, which she had done a few times in the last five minutes. Cain thought it was because she was studying something interesting on the screen, until he saw her rub her eyes.

The screen was blurry for her. Probably because of exhaustion. But she just kept soldiering on.

And she would continue to do that until she fell over from exhaustion.

Fighting for her against even her own inclinations. Steve was right.

Cain opened the door. "Time for a break."

Hayley didn't even turn to look at him. "I'm okay. I ate a couple hours ago."

He walked straight up to her chair and wheeled it back from the desk.

"Hey." Her brown eyes peered up at him.

"Time for a break."

She let out a sigh. "A break is not going to help me. Finding out who's trying to kill me and attacking our son…that will help me."

Cain crouched down so that he was directly in front of Hayley's line of sight. "Mason is very well protected right now. You were shot a day and a half ago and haven't gotten much rest. The nights before that you were either in a car or in a cell about to be sent back to prison. I know you didn't get much sleep in, either."

Her small hand came up and rubbed the back of her neck. "That's true, but—"

He reached over and kissed her forehead. "Six hours of sleep, that's what I'm asking of you. You and I both know that what you're doing now—trying to work without all your cylinders firing—might cause you to miss something." Not to mention collapse on the floor.

"But—"

"Work's over for today."

"Just one more hour…"

Cain bent down, sliding his arms under her knees and around her back, and picked her up bodily from the chair. She let out a surprised squeak before her arms flew around his neck.

"No 'one more hour.' Because in an hour, you'll want another one. You need rest."

This close to her he was able to see the dark circles under her eyes, the exhaustion bracketing her mouth.

He should've made her rest long before now. Steve was right. Cain didn't need to tell Hayley she was important to him, he needed to *show* her.

"I'm really not that tired—" Her words were cut off by the huge yawn that overtook her.

Cain raised an eyebrow. "You were saying?"

"Fine." Her pout was adorable. "Just get me to a couch. I'm sure I'll be able to crash there just fine."

He gently set her on her feet in front of him at the door, wrapped an arm around her waist and led her out into the hall. The door automatically locked behind them.

"There's a studio apartment here in the complex especially for situations like this. Steve got it set up for us."

She was almost asleep on her feet by the time he got them to the room. He led her over to the bed and sat her down so he could bend to untie her shoes and slip them off. Then his hands moved to the snap of her jeans.

"Let's get these off you, too. You'll be more comfortable."

It took every ounce of control Cain had to just peel

Hayley's jeans off, not touching any of the smooth skin of her legs. He got them off and was setting them to the side when he felt Hayley's fingers on his arm.

"Stay with me," she whispered.

He wanted to. More than anything he wanted to. "If I get in that bed right now, you are not going to get the sleep you need."

The corners of her lips rose in a temptress's smile, blond hair spilling on the pillow all around her. Beguiling. Enchanting. His heart thundered in his chest.

"Hayley…" His voice was husky even to his own ears. He sat down on the bed beside her.

Her hand reached out for him again. "I'll get the sleep I need. It just won't be right away."

Cain stared at her. He wanted to do what was right in this situation, but damned if he knew what that was. "I didn't bring you here for this. For sex. You're exhausted."

"And you don't want to take advantage of me."

"Yes, exactly."

She sat up and hooked an arm around the back of his neck, pulling him closer. "Then how about if I take advantage of you. Multiple times."

Her lips met his. Hot, wet, open. Cain didn't even try to resist. His hands slipped into her hair and he pushed her back against the pillows, mindful of her wound, and devoured her. He couldn't hide the affect she had on him. Didn't even try.

He'd waited so long for this. *They'd* waited.

Pleasure arced through him. He swallowed her sigh as their tongues dueled, mated. He felt her fingers gripping his hair, keeping him close.

As if he were going anywhere else.

Cain eased his weight more fully on top of her, keeping off her injured side. He moaned as he felt one of her legs move up to wrap around his hips. Everything about this was right. This was Hayley. He'd been so empty without her.

He pulled back from their kiss, just needing to look at her face.

Eyes hooded, lips swollen from his kisses, hair tousled. He wasn't sure he'd ever seen anything as beautiful as how she looked right now.

"Everything okay?" she asked.

"Perfect," he said.

And he proceeded to show her.

Chapter Eighteen

"I'm such an idiot."

Cain responded from where he sat in the other room. "You have the highest IQ of anyone I know. You're very definitely not an idiot, and you're going to lose a couple more hours of work if I have to drag you back to bed and prove that to you."

She was glad he couldn't see her face since she could feel the heat rising in her cheeks.

She could feel heat rising in other places, too. Especially after last night.

The lovemaking between them had always been passionate, burning hot through them both. Last night they'd had a much different perspective than they'd had when they were teenagers. Both aware of how easily love could be lost. And how precious it was when it was in your grasp.

And although the passion had still burned just as hot, it had been undergirded with a tenderness and sense of being cherished. Nothing taken for granted.

"No, I think that got proven plenty last night," she

said. And this morning. "But I said that because I think I've figured out how to draw out whoever is trying to kill me, and it's so simple. I've just been looking at it the wrong way."

Cain came and sat down next to her. He'd been doing that on and off all day. She wasn't sure if it was to provide moral support or to double-check what she was doing because even after last night a part of him still didn't trust her.

She was afraid to ask which.

"Since the trapdoor I set before I was arrested didn't gather much useful information, I've been trying other algorithms to see if I could figure out the pattern of the people using the CET exams for espionage."

"But no luck."

"Nothing. If they were smart they stopped once they found out someone was onto them. Or they may have just changed their patterns altogether. In that case, my finding them again the same way I did the first time would be a matter of sheer blind luck."

"But you figured out another way."

Hayley nodded, then brought a new set of figures up on the screen. "I don't need to find the seller. I can find the buyers."

"In the foreign countries."

"Yes. There have to be people allowed in to take these tests who are unusual in some way. I highly doubt they've recruited high school students from US Department of Defense schools on foreign soil."

Cain leaned forward to look more clearly at the screen and data she'd pulled up. "Maybe in a couple of the schools, but definitely not in all of them."

"The computer will filter out most of the kids and will pull files based on the criteria I've set for red-flagging—not being a US citizen, over eighteen years old or any ties to criminals in any country. We should have a list of people by the end of the day."

"You have access to that information?"

Maybe she should've asked him before pulling in all the law enforcement systems for her algorithms.

"Not me personally." She hesitated. "But Omega Sector, combined with the FBI and Interpol, do."

His face turned grim. "Did you just hack law enforcement databases from all over the world?"

She shrugged, not looking at him. "Technically I only had to open myself a window into the Omega system. You guys already had access to the other law enforcement and I could run it through you."

Cain ran a hand over his face.

"I'm not going to apologize for using every available resource I can access. Not when it comes to keeping my son safe."

"*Our* son."

She looked at him now. "Our son. Even more so. I would think you would understand that."

He rubbed his face again. "I do. It's just…"

"It's just you don't know if you can fully trust me."

He didn't say anything for a long moment. Finally

he sat back in his chair. "You're right. I want to do whatever has to be done to keep you and Mason safe."

But that still didn't address the issue of trust. Which stung considering what they'd shared last night.

They worked in silence for the next few hours while the computer was running her program to sort out suspects. Hayley moved her attention to the Omega mole. Cain didn't put pressure on her to explain anything she was working on or justify any methods, but she noticed he never wandered far from where she was working.

Trust again?

The pressure of it seemed to crash down on her. Cain had never spoken about the future—with her or Mason—not even last night in the midst of their physical intimacy. Maybe he didn't plan on a real future.

And if he did, how could they even consider it when he was never going to be able to trust her again?

Hayley took her hands off the keyboard and put them in her lap.

"What's wrong?" Cain asked immediately.

"I want to see Mason." She hadn't seen her son in two days. Heaven knew she had gone much longer than that without seeing him, but right now with everything that was going on, and the world spiraling out of control, she wanted to see her son.

"Right now?" Cain asked.

She nodded, preparing herself for all the arguments he was going to make. That the work she was doing was more important than spending time with her child. That every minute not spent trying to catch the people selling secrets of the United States, the more dangerous it was for everyone, including Mason.

But instead Cain just nodded. "Okay. Give me a few minutes to set it up."

Tears pricked her eyes. His willingness to understand her need to see Mason meant a lot. She touched Cain on his arm as he was grabbing his cell phone. "I—thank you."

His fingers trailed down her cheeks. "Your needs matter, too. God knows you spent long enough without him."

Just when she thought there could be no future for them, he went and said something like that.

Gathering Mason into her arms an hour later, Hayley felt like she could breathe again. Just seeing his little face, feeling the fierceness of his hug, reassured the mother's heart in her.

He hadn't forgotten her. She always worried that he would. Intellectually she knew he wouldn't, but it was still hard to convince herself of that when her fears began to press in all around her.

But when she held him, all the fear melted away and the truth couldn't be denied: Mason loved her.

He squeezed her and gave her a wet kiss on the cheek until he saw Cain.

"Candy Cain!" Mason climbed from her over to Cain and began chattering about riding the roller coaster again. It took her a minute to realize what Mason meant.

Cain still hadn't quite figured it out, even though Mason kept pressing him. He looked questioningly at Hayley.

"He wants to ride the roller coaster again. You know, leap across a rooftop at full speed."

Cain threw back his head and laughed. "I don't know about that, buddy," he said to Mason. "But I'll bet we can find some other roller coasters to go on."

Cain flipped Mason onto his belly in his arms and flew him around the room. Mason's giggles could be heard all over the house. Hayley gave a quick hug to Ariel and shook the hands of Summer and Ashton, thanking them once again for allowing Mason to stay with them.

"It's really no problem. Chloe loves him and he's very gentle with her."

Hayley looked over to where Cain now had Mason tucked up under one arm and Chloe, who evidently hadn't wanted to be left out of the action, tucked under the other, flying them around the living room.

Cain would make such an amazing father. No matter what happened between the two of them—whether her heart ended in a bloody, broken state as she was afraid it would—Hayley would never try to keep Cain from Mason's life. She would be doing both of them a grave injustice.

"I understand you're trying to help bring down the mole inside Omega Sector." Summer came to stand next to Hayley as she watched Cain play with the children.

"Yes. I'm trying."

"Whoever the traitor is almost killed me, Ashton *and* Chloe. So when I say that we will make sure your family is safe so you can do your job, I mean it. Nothing is more important to us than catching whoever is behind these attacks."

"We're getting closer every day."

Summer slid an arm around Hayley's back and gave a little squeeze. Her smile was as bright as her name. "You don't strike me as the hugging type, but I wanted to do that anyway. I know it must be hard being away from Mason. And nothing makes up for Mommy not being here, but I promise we will protect him."

"Thank you."

Summer's words were enough, were everything to Hayley. This woman knew what it was like to have the ones she loved most targeted. Hayley could go back to Omega now, secure in the knowledge that Mason and Ariel were truly out of harm's way.

It was time to catch a killer.

Chapter Nineteen

"Cain, I've got something."

It was the next morning. Hayley had insisted on working all night after they'd returned from seeing Mason. He'd tried to talk her into stopping for rest, or even other things, but she was moving forward with a purpose now.

He could only admire it.

Her program was still narrowing CET exam takers in foreign countries. The first round of results had given them a group of suspects too broad, so she'd had to reset the parameters and run it again.

"CET case or the mole?" he asked.

"Mole. I've got a name."

"What?" Cain rushed to her side now.

She grimaced. "Not a real name, unfortunately. I've just discovered he calls himself Fawkes."

"Fawkes? As in Guy Fawkes, the British guy who attempted to blow up the government a couple hundred years ago?"

"I would assume so, especially based on what I found."

He sat down next to her. "Show me."

"It doesn't help with identification, but it's definitely something set up by him. Or her. And it wasn't meant to be found. At least not this early."

"What is it?"

She brought up a picture on a screen, with the name of a file.

Manifesto of Change.

"What the hell?" Hayley opened the file and Cain began to read.

"'On my honor, I will never betray my badge, my integrity, my character or the public trust.

"'I will always have the courage to hold myself and others accountable for our actions.

"'I will always uphold the constitution, my community and the agency I serve.'"

Cain looked over at her. "That's the Oath of Honor law enforcement officers take at their swearing-in ceremony." He continued reading out loud.

"'We all took an oath to uphold the law, but instead we have allowed the public to make a mockery of it. Where is the honor, the integrity, the character in not using the privilege and power given to us by our training and station to wipe clean those who would infect our society? We were meant to rise up, to be an example to the people, to control them when needed in order to make a more perfect civilization.

"'But we are weak. Afraid of popular opinion whenever force must be used. So now we have changed the configuration of law enforcement forever.

"'And now, only now, will you truly understand what it means to hold yourselves accountable for your actions. Only with death is life truly appreciated. Only with violence can true change be propagated. As we build anew, let us not make the same mistakes. Let the badge mean something again.

"'Let the badge rule as it was meant to do.'"

Cain stared at the screen, reading the manifesto again silently before whistling through his teeth. "That's some pretty extreme stuff. Calling for a police state. For a law enforcement ruling class."

Hayley nodded. "And history wasn't my best subject, but it's pretty ironic that the mole chose the name Fawkes. Fawkes was trying to destroy the government to give the *people* more power."

"This guy is doing the exact opposite." Cain read the words again. "Can you tell when it's set to release?"

"I'm trying to nail down the date, but I can't. But it's for soon, Cain." Her brows knitted. "Maybe even in the next couple of weeks."

Cain cursed under his breath. "Who will it release to?"

"Everyone at Omega Sector, for sure." She typed a few commands into the keyboard and a flowchart came up on the second screen. "And it looks like it is set to then automatically forward to every other law enforcement agency Omega Sector is connected to."

"After some huge, violent event that we don't know."

"That obviously targets law enforcement in some way." She bit her lip. "And worse, because I know you're close with Ashton and some of the others, but this message is linked to someone on the Omega SWAT team."

Cain's curse was even more foul. "How certain are you?"

"Given the fact that the mole doesn't know I'm in the system? Almost completely."

"Do you know who?"

"No, because the mole routed the information through almost every login ID on the SWAT team. Which was smart. Implicates everyone."

Cain thought of John Carnell and Saul Poniard, both of whom had caught his attention when he'd first been brought in for investigation. Carnell was a genius and definitely had the ability to do the computer dirty work Hayley was suggesting. Poniard was a power-hungry SWAT wannabe who had been reprimanded more than once for unnecessary use of force.

"There's only one SWAT team member whose ID wasn't used in the routing," Hayley said. "Someone named Muir. I don't know why. He might've just been overlooked or it's possible that Muir was skipped on purpose. Given that we accessed this information before the traitor meant to send it, I would start investigating this guy Muir as soon as possible."

"Gal."

"What?"

"Lillian Muir is a woman. The only female on the SWAT team."

And another one who'd been on top of Cain's *suspicious* pile. Given her history that she'd gone through so much trouble to hide, this Manifesto of Change could definitely be her brainchild.

Cain stood. "I've got to get this information to Steve so we can run it against upcoming events and possible terrorist attacks."

"Okay. I'll just keep working here. I should be able to manually eliminate some of these CET suspects my program is red-flagging."

Cain hesitated for just a second. He would be leaving her here, unprotected, knowing that the mole—*Fawkes*—was also in this building and would kill her if given a chance.

Also knowing he would be leaving her here with full, unfettered access to a computer.

But damn it, he needed to get this info to Steve, so he could begin making contingencies. That couldn't be done here.

"Okay," he said. "I'll be back soon. Stay in here and keep the door locked."

Hayley's look was shuttered as she turned back to her computer. Obviously his hesitation hadn't been lost on her. Tension knotted Cain's shoulders as he walked to the outer door. There never seemed to be any easy solutions when he was with Hayley.

He turned back before he left. "It's your safety I'm concerned about, too. Okay?"

"But it's also about what you're afraid I might do while you're gone."

"I'm leaving you here so I'm obviously not that afraid." And he realized it was true. He would prefer it if he could stay by her side every time she was at a computer, since that's what he'd agreed to in the original parole easement agreement. But it was more because he wanted to be able to say he'd lived up to his end of the agreement than it was because he thought she was going to do something bad if left unsupervised.

She nodded, looking back at him. "Fair enough."

Fair enough.

That was just it, wasn't it? He and Hayley had to figure out their balance together. What was fair. What they wanted. How they fit together.

Cain walked back over to Hayley and leaned down to her. He cupped her face and brought his lips to the generous curves of her mouth. What he'd meant as a light kiss turned deeper. A fire licked at them both, and when he pulled away they both were breathing heavily.

"We have things to work out. And we will," he said.

"Everything feels so shaky sometimes."

He nipped at her bottom lip. "That kiss didn't feel shaky."

Her soft, sweet laugh wrapped its way around his heart. "No, it sure didn't."

He straightened and turned back toward the door.

He really did need to get this Manifesto of Change info to Steve immediately.

"I'll be back soon. Stay out of trouble."

HAYLEY BROKE THE order to stay out of trouble in the worst possible way. Fortified with another mug of coffee, she dived into the CET case. She found a pattern an hour later. Confirmed it long after that.

Ran it one more time to be sure.

She shot back from her computer as if that would protect her from the information. She'd known it was someone pretty powerful who was selling the secrets. But she'd had no idea the link between the buyers would be a US senator.

Not only that, Senator Ralph Nelligar had been one of most vocal detractors of the CET exam system over the years. He was one of the people who had called for a speedy trial of the hackers, arguing that this sort of electronic exposure was what he'd been afraid of from the beginning.

Proving that Senator Nelligar was the one selling state secrets by using the test would be almost impossible. All Hayley had right now were vague links between his office and questionable people who'd taken the CET on foreign soil. Definitely not enough to convict the senator. Hayley was lucky she had someone like Cain who believed her at all.

Even worse, the senator had the resources to find Hayley and Mason, no matter where they hid. He was obviously the one behind making her parole documents disappear from the system and her rapid re-arrest and arraignment. Hayley wouldn't be able to outrun him and his resources.

Maybe—*maybe*—Hayley might be able to build up enough evidence of the situation to scare the senator into stopping his actions. But she doubted she'd ever be able to prove it was him. Especially now that he knew she was the one who knew his secret. Cain wouldn't be able to help, either.

She was still just staring blankly at the screen, trying to figure out what in the world she was going to do, when Cain returned. She had no idea how long he'd been gone.

He took one look at her face and sat in the chair beside her. "What?"

She told him what she'd discovered. That all the paths were leading back to Senator Nelligar.

His low curse pretty much echoed everything she felt about the situation.

"I know," she whispered. "I know this is a lot and your plate is already full with what we found out about Fawkes. I just don't know what to do."

Cain rubbed the back of his neck. "We'll see if we can figure out some way to set a trap."

Hayley nodded, but she doubted the senator would be dumb enough to fall for one. Not knowing she was looking for him.

"Meanwhile," Cain continued, "we're going to need to put you and Mason into protective custody."

"Last I checked, law enforcement wouldn't put a known fugitive in protective custody."

"Yeah, we'll have to work around that. I'll talk to Steve. We can work something out, even if it's temporary. But for right now, at least for a few days, you, Mason and Ariel are safe at Ashton and Summer's place. You have no ties to them and there's no official record of it."

"Yeah, we definitely need to remember that whoever is doing Senator Nelligar's electronic dirty work is good. Very good."

"As good as you?"

"Maybe." She shrugged a shoulder wearily. "The point is, we should work under the assumption that nearly any information put into a networked computer can be hacked by Senator Nelligar."

Cain nodded. "Got it."

"I should do more work now, but it seems pointless until I come up with some sort of plan."

He slipped an arm around her shoulders and kissed her temple. "We know who the bad guy is. That gives us a huge upper hand. Now we just need to wait for him to make a mistake, or even better, do something to cause him to rush into one."

"But I don't know what that is." Her brain was tired. She needed to get away from screens and keyboards. "Let me go rest in the apartment. That will help."

"How about if I take you to Summer and Ashton's. Be with Mason and Ariel. Get rest there." He held out a hand. "And before you even think it, this is not about not trusting you. You need a break from this."

She reached her hand up to twine her fingers with his. "What about you? You need a break, too."

"And I'll get one. Just not yet. Not with what you found about Fawkes and his damned manifesto."

"What did Steve think?"

"Same as us. That Fawkes has a big explosion planned and that this is his love letter regarding it. Problem is, without knowing who Fawkes is, we can't get as many agents focused on this as we normally would."

"Too big a chance of us tipping him off that we're onto him. I'm sorry I couldn't get a positive ID. He, or she, is pretty clever."

Cain trailed his fingers down her cheek and she couldn't help but lean into the touch slightly. "What you found is going to save a lot of lives. You take a break. Let Steve and me do some work. You can come back tomorrow and look at it all with fresh eyes."

Hayley prayed it would make a difference.

Chapter Twenty

Cain had been right: everything seemed not so over-whelming when she woke the next day, after ten hours of sleep, Mason running in to ask if she wanted pancakes.

"Kiss first," she said.

He scrunched up his little face, but then kissed her before running back into the kitchen. Hayley could hear Ariel and Summer in there with him and Chloe.

She got dressed and ran a brush through her hair—good thing about prison had been the elimination of a lot of unnecessary beauty habits—checked the dressing on her wound, and made her way out to help.

"There she is, just in time!" Ariel gave her a huge smile. "You look so much better."

"Thanks. I feel it. Looks like a feast in here."

Summer grinned. "We had two aspiring chefs." She set out a tray of pancakes and put Chloe into her high chair. Hayley helped Mason into his booster seat.

"Ashton's not here?" she asked.

"No, he got called in to work." Summer gave her a direct look. "A project only certain people can work on."

So he was helping Steve and Cain with the info about Fawkes. Good. They needed all the people they could trust working on this.

It was only a few minutes later when Summer's cell phone rang. After talking into it for just a minute she handed it to Hayley.

"Cain wants to talk to you."

She took it. "Hello?"

"We've got to get you your own phone. I've got to get a new one, too. This burner has outlived its purpose."

"Yeah. There's a lot I need to start thinking about if we're going to be here long-term."

"I know you're supposed to have a full twenty-four hours off, but we think we might be onto something and I was wondering if you could come in."

"Sure."

"Okay," he said. "I'll be there to get you in about forty-five minutes."

"Why don't I just drive if Summer doesn't mind my borrowing her car?" Summer nodded from across the table, giving her an okay sign with her fingers. "It's a waste of time for you to come all the way out here just to go all the way back. Nobody knows I'm here, so it's got to be safe."

She heard Cain say something to someone else before talking to her again. "Yeah, that would be good. Evidently I have someone here to see me anyway."

"I'll call you as soon as I'm in the building."

Hayley hated to leave Mason again, but Summer assured her he was fine and welcome. Hayley provided a bit of information about what was going on, and the possibility of witness protection for her and Mason. To be honest, Hayley wasn't exactly sure what it would mean for Ariel and her upcoming plans for Oxford.

But as always, her cousin hugged her and told her they would figure it out.

As Hayley pulled out of the subdivision she tried to work through what this new change was really going to mean. Would Ariel be safe to go to Oxford? Would Senator Nelligar go after her to try to get to Hayley?

If she could take it all back, never accidentally stumble upon those dark activities, she would do it. She would do just about anything to keep her loved ones safe.

And she had to admit to herself that now included Cain.

She stopped at a red light, trying to come to grips with those feelings—

When the passenger door was flung open and someone got inside her car.

"Oh God." It took Hayley a second to realize what was going on. But before she could unbuckle her seat belt and fling herself out the door, she saw the gun pointed at her.

"Light just turned green. I need you to drive, Hayley."

Hayley's eyes flew to the woman holding the gun, her voice familiar yet different.

She did a double take. *"Mara?"*

The woman looked different, her hair no longer as teased and poufy as when she'd worked at the Bluewater. Her voice was different, Southern accent gone. Even her posture had changed—more domineering, self-assured.

"Drive, Hayley."

Somebody honked behind them, but Hayley still couldn't make herself move the vehicle. What was Mara doing in the car pointing a gun at her?

"Hayley." Mara gave a big sigh. "If you don't move the car my next call is going to be to have someone go point a gun at your son."

That got her driving immediately. She took off through the intersection.

"What are you doing here?"

"I know for a fact you're not that dumb, Hayley. Figure it out."

Hayley knew that the woman was obviously here due to one of the cases. What she didn't know was which one.

"Senator Nelligar sent you?"

"Actually, no."

"Fawkes?" She just kept driving straight, no idea where she was going.

"What the hell is Fawkes?"

So not the traitor inside Omega. "So the senator did send you."

"No, the senator has no idea I'm here. Has no idea anything is going on at all."

Hayley wanted to bang her head against the steering wheel. All the clues had led her to Senator Nelligar's office, so she'd assumed the man himself was behind the crimes of treason. But really it could've been any of his close assistants. Anyone who had access to the information and his computer network.

"You work in his office." It wasn't a question.

"Yep. I've been his aide for eight years now, although I'm on a temporary leave of absence to take care of some 'family issues.'" Mara used her fingers to make air quotes for the last two words.

"How did you find me?"

"You were nice enough to call me back a few days ago. Once I had the details from that phone I was able to track it. It was used again today. I couldn't get inside Omega Sector, but it was easy to track where the call went. Turn left here."

Hayley did what she said, not wanting to take a chance that Mara would send someone after Mason, especially since Ashton wasn't home.

"Having to chase you across the country wasn't what I had planned. I still haven't figured out how you got out of the fire at the restaurant."

"Cain," Hayley muttered.

"Of course. Big Omega agent swooped in to your rescue."

"He wasn't even there for you or anything to do with the CET. He needed my help with another case."

Mara blew out an irritated breath. "We couldn't take that chance. As soon as your name showed up for a court order to get your computer privileges reinstated we knew you had to go. Although honestly I didn't think it was you who had figured out our little scheme."

Which was why so many of the other hackers had died and Hayley was still alive.

"Turn right at the next light."

Mara was leading her toward the outskirts of town, Hayley realized. Somewhere she could get rid of her quietly.

"I'm not just going to let you drive me somewhere so you can shoot me and dump my body, Mara."

"Oh, trust me, I'm not going to shoot you. That would be way too suspicious. Besides, we need you and Agent Bennett to die together in order for this story to work."

Mara had Hayley turn again, this time into a parking lot for a three-story office building. A huge sign hanging on the front said the building was for rent.

"What is this?" Hayley said after Mara made her get out of the car with the gun.

"An empty office building," Mara said as if that

explained everything. "This is where we're going to wait for Agent Bennett to show up."

Mara led Hayley through the door and up the elevator to the third floor. She opened a set of doors and pushed Hayley through. The space was wide and empty except for a desk with a computer that sat over near the window.

Hayley didn't know why Mara had brought her here, but it couldn't be good. She did know this might be her only chance to get away, so Hayley was going to take it.

She waited until she could feel Mara close behind her, then spun and knocked the gun out of the other woman's hands. Then it became a fight to see who could reach the weapon first. Mara dived for it but Hayley plowed into her, gasping as she felt her stitches tear from the wound at her waist.

Hayley elbowed Mara in the midsection and scrambled for the gun when the other woman doubled over, and had her finger on the tip of it, but Mara caught her leg and pulled her back. A second later Hayley cried out through the starburst of agony as Mara dug her knee into Hayley's wound. Hayley fell to the ground, gasping for air, and Mara was able to get to the weapon.

Blood was already soaking Hayley's shirt as Mara turned the gun on her again from where she sat breathing heavily on the floor.

"You know, you're really starting to piss me off.

You're lucky we need you and Bennett to be here when you both die or else you'd be dead already."

Careful to keep her distance this time, Mara gestured to the office chair by the desk and computer. "Sit there and don't give me any grief or you'll know what it's like to be shot twice in one week."

Hayley got off the ground, trying to resituate the bandage over her wound to help stop the bleeding. Handcuffs with one metal circle already linked around the chair's armrest handle hung to the side.

"Cuff yourself to the chair."

"I need my arm to be able to deal with my wound."

Mara laughed, an ugly, bitter sound that filled Hayley with dread. "Believe me, that wound is going to be the least of your problems." She pointed the gun at Hayley's kneecap. "Cuffs, or I make sure you can't run."

Hayley clinked the metal band around her wrist. Mara lowered the gun and tightened it, then fastened her other wrist with a second set of cuffs.

"Now what?" Hayley asked.

"Now we wait for Agent Bennett to show up. Shouldn't take very long."

"I won't call him. I won't lead him into a trap." Hayley prayed they wouldn't use Mason against her to make her lead Cain to his death.

Mara leaned back against the desk and stretched her legs out in front of her. "Oh, you won't have to call him. He'll come on his own."

"To rescue me? Do you really think that's a good

idea? Cain works with one of the greatest law enforcement groups on the planet. You really think they won't be able to rescue me when they figure out I've been kidnapped?"

"Oh, sweetheart." Mara tsked and Hayley wondered how she could've ever liked the woman. "He won't be coming here to rescue you, he'll be coming here to arrest you."

"What?"

"Even right now Agent Bennett is being notified of this location. Where you and a couple of your hacker buddies have been participating in a few extracurricular actives of the illegal variety."

"Oh my God."

"Yeah. We knew we wouldn't be able to get Agent Bennett here alone by kidnapping you. Like you said, we'd be no match for Omega Sector. But how do you think he's going to feel when he's given irrefutable proof that you've been lying to him?"

Hayley jerked against the handcuffs and Mara laughed.

"Been lying to him about the boy. About the hacking. About the CET. Proof that you were just using Bennett as the fool who could get you unlimited computer access, so you could continue your espionage and blame it on poor Senator Nelligar."

Mara turned and walked closer, grinning. Hayley wanted to claw the other woman's eyes out.

"A representative from Senator Nelligar's office fortunately became aware of your dirty deeds and has brought the info to Bennett. He's hoping Cain will be willing to take you in without a huge scene. Nobody wants this to get into the press's hands."

"So Cain will come here to arrest me." Bile itched at the back of Hayley's throat.

"And won't it be a shame when you both die in the process of that arrest?"

Chapter Twenty-One

Cain wasn't particularly interested in meeting whoever was waiting for him in the lobby of the Omega
HQ. The name—Joshua Lawson—had not rung any
bells, nor had the man stated why he was here when
he had someone call for Cain.

Cain had a ton of stuff to do, not the least of which
was helping Ashton and Steve sort through the possible targets Fawkes might be considering. Plus, Hayley would be back in a few minutes and he needed
to be with her as she ran down some possibilities
for where Fawkes might be planning his—or her—
attack.

When the lobby guard pointed Lawson out, Cain
walked briskly over to the man dressed in a suit
that was probably more expensive than all of Cain's
combined.

"Mr. Lawson. I'm Agent Bennett. What can I do
for you?"

Lawson shook Cain's outstretched hand. "I was
wondering if I might have a few moments of your

time to discuss a case you were the lead agent for a few years ago."

Cain very definitely did not have time to discuss old cases right now.

"Mr. Lawson, I am really very sorry, but today I am totally swamped with something that is of a critical and timely nature."

Cain didn't want to dismiss the other man's concerns, whatever they were. But he couldn't deal with them today. "Would it be possible for you to come back next week? Plus I can give you the number of my office assistant and she can go ahead and pull the files for me so I can be better prepared to answer any questions you might have."

Lawson didn't look like he was going anywhere. "The case I need to speak with you about involves Hayley Green."

Cain's eyes narrowed. "I'm sorry, I didn't get who you represented or what this was about."

"I work for Senator Ralph Nelligar. We've gotten hold of some very interesting information that I think you will want to see. Preferably not here in the lobby."

The man who had offered a reward to have Hayley killed, who was committing treason by selling state secrets to foreign countries, was sending someone to talk to Cain *inside his own headquarters*?

Cain didn't know where the hell this was going, but he was definitely going to ride it out. Maybe Hayley wouldn't need to set a trap for Senator Nelligar. Maybe he was setting one for himself right now.

But it was definitely important that she not come waltzing through the door in case Mr. Lawson wasn't here alone. She could be arrested immediately.

"Can you wait here for a minute while I get us a conference room?" Lawson nodded and Cain grabbed the phone at the guard's desk to call Steve.

"Drackett."

"Steve, it's Cain. I'm in the lobby with a representative from Senator Nelligar's office."

Cain had already filled Steve in on what Hayley had found with the CET situation. "That seems pretty risky for someone in danger of being arrested for treason."

"I'm going to hear what the guy has to say. See if we can get Nelligar to hang himself. Hayley's on her way in, actually should've already been in by now. I'll need you to waylay her while I'm meeting with this guy in case this is a fishing expedition."

If Cain had to guess why Lawson was here, it was to figure out where Hayley was, so they could take her out.

"Will do. I'll set up conference room two for you."

Cain led Lawson to the conference room after his briefcase and person were scanned for any dangers. He shut the door behind them and sat down at the table.

"I know you said you are busy, so I won't waste

your time, Agent Bennett. I need to talk to you about Hayley Green."

"What about her?"

"You are aware that Ms. Green is a fugitive, correct? She was last seen at your family's home when she was arrested."

Looked like this *was* a fishing expedition. "Yes, I am, and yes, she was. But she was brought into custody by Georgia law enforcement."

"And escaped," Lawson said. "But really that's not my point. We know Ms. Green has been…working with you."

"If the question you're ultimately asking is if Hayley Green is here, then the answer is no, she's not. Omega Sector and their agents do not make a practice of harboring fugitives."

All true, technically speaking.

Lawson smiled, and something about it made Cain's gut clench.

"We know where Ms. Green is. We also know there's a connection between the two of you that is very strong."

Cain wanted to stop and call Steve, see if Hayley had arrived yet. Because he very definitely did not like Lawson's assuredness about Hayley's location.

Cain leaned back in his chair, not giving away the panic itching at his throat. "Well, sounds like you know a lot of stuff. Which also probably means you know that someone is trying to kill Hayley. That a hit has been put out on her life." Cain watched the other man closely as he said it. Would Lawson try to deny it?

He didn't. "Yes, it would seem that way, especially to you."

"To me?"

"Agent Bennett, we have reason to believe that Hayley Green is the one who put the 'hit' on her own life."

Cain rolled his eyes. "So you're saying she wanted to pay someone to kill her."

"I'm saying she wanted to pay someone to make *you* think someone was trying to kill her."

"Is that so? And the fact that Hayley was *shot* by the would-be assassins at one point?" Cain knew he was giving away a little information, but knew he could cover if needed.

"A life-threatening wound?" Lawson asked.

Cain grit his teeth. "No." As a matter of fact he remembered thinking that as far as getting shot went, Hayley couldn't have possibly taken a bullet in a better place.

Lawson raised an eyebrow. "Let me ask you this. Did getting shot cause you to trust Hayley more or less?"

Cain didn't respond. He hadn't thought of her wound in terms of trust level.

Lawson took a different tack when Cain didn't answer. "You arrested Ms. Green nearly four and a half years ago with the CET hacking case."

"That's correct."

"What if I told you that I have proof that she was using the hacking to hide even more nefarious activities? And now that she's out of prison she's interested in resuming those activities—using you to gain early access to a computer without bringing law enforcement down on her."

Cain could feel tension creeping into his body at the other man's words. "I would say that sounds pretty far-fetched."

Lawson took sets of printouts from his briefcase. "I think this will provide proof of Ms. Green's questionable activities."

Cain sat as Lawson explained each paper. Showing him how someone had accessed the CET system again, for certain foreign countries like Hayley had been studying, but through a back door.

"Just like someone would do if they were going to say, sell secrets, using the exam."

"I agree it's suspicious." Cain now held the paper in his hands. "But this doesn't prove anything about Hayley."

Lawson pointed out numbers on each set of papers. "These are the Internet protocol addresses—or as you and I would call them, IP addresses—for the actions. I think if you looked it up, the first set are for your laptop computer and the second set are for a computer here within Omega Sector."

Cain wasn't sure what the IP address was for the computer here, but he did know his laptop. It was the same number.

And the dates and times recorded in the printouts were the very ones when Cain had felt like Hayley had been trying to sneak something by him. That her actions seemed suspicious. He'd wondered if she'd been trying to reconnect with the hackers she'd worked with. Then he'd decided it was just her nervousness concerning Cain finding out about Mason.

But looking at it now, it seemed like very damning evidence indeed.

The other dates and times were definitely at points where she'd been working at Omega HQ, sometimes completely unsupervised.

Cain wanted to rip the papers into shreds and throw Lawson bodily from the building. Wanted to pummel the other man. But that wouldn't solve the problem.

He couldn't believe this was happening again. Worse.

"Agent Bennett, we know you and Ms. Green had—*have*—a personal relationship. I can certainly understand how you would not want to believe that someone you've been intimate with could betray you and your country in such a way. Treason."

His personal feelings for Hayley had nothing to do with the situation at hand. He was about to tell Lawson when he slid across another set of papers.

"As you know, Ms. Green gave birth to a child while at the Georgia Women's Correctional Institute about four years ago."

Cain definitely did not want to talk about Mason

with this man. Especially not with what he'd just told Cain about Hayley. But he finally looked down at the papers Lawson continued to slide across the table at him.

Every ounce of blood drained from his face when he saw what they were.

"Complete blood work and DNA testing is done on any child born within the prison system of Georgia. For insurance purposes."

Cain couldn't believe what Lawson had given him to read.

"So, as you can see. Your DNA and the child's do not match. So you could not be biologically related to that child. I don't know that Ms. Green would've implied that you were. But in hopes that this makes your decision easier, we wanted to make sure you knew the truth."

Cain didn't want to look at the papers anymore. He folded them. "Do you mind if I keep these?"

Lawson gave a sympathetic nod. "Certainly. You might want to look it over more closely later."

The more compassionate Lawson looked the more Cain wanted to punch him. But it wouldn't do any good. Wouldn't change the past or anything that needed to happen now.

Cain could see exactly where he fell as a player in a very elaborate game.

It was time to end it.

"Why are you coming to me with this? What do you want me to do?"

"I'm not in law enforcement," Lawson said. "So I can't make an arrest. I don't want to lead regular police to where she is in case it gives Green a chance to warn the people she's been in contact with. And I certainly don't want the press involved."

Cain just nodded.

"These are very dangerous secrets she's been selling. Weapon and gun schematics as well as other valuable intel. Items that will give enemies of the United States the upper hand. Cost the lives of American soldiers."

Cain just wanted this to be over. "Where is she?"

"I'll take you to her. Right now, if that works for you. Then you can make sure she's put away for good."

Cain wiped a hand over his face and nodded. This was his chance to take control. To end this once and for all. He hardened himself against any thoughts of gentleness for Hayley. This wasn't going to be easy for either of them.

"I just need five minutes to line up a few things." Cain rubbed the back of his neck. "And to pull myself together." Cain felt like the papers with Mason's DNA results were burning a hole in his pocket.

Lawson nodded with understanding. "Sure. This is all pretty difficult to digest."

Cain just nodded. It didn't matter how difficult it was. He had a job to do.

Chapter Twenty-Two

Hayley sat handcuffed to the chair, desperate to try to find a way to contact Cain. He was going to walk into a trap and they were both going to die.

Mara had delighted in telling Hayley all the "evidence" her colleague was showing Cain right now. They were so clever, printing documents to make it look like Hayley had been the one selling state secrets. Making it look just real enough to be possible.

Once Cain was presented with this proof, Hayley wouldn't blame him for believing them. They'd done a damn good job of making it seem like Hayley had strung Cain along just to get access to a computer.

Mara and whoever else she was working with obviously knew their way around a computer. They were good. Their evidence was nearly flawless. Especially when Cain had never been able to get past his innate mistrust of Hayley to begin with.

Mara and Company had basically just given Cain a push in the direction his brain and instincts already had wanted to take him anyway.

"What if he doesn't buy it?" Hayley asked, hoping beyond all hope it would be true. She didn't want both of them to die here in this empty set of offices.

She didn't want to die here alone, either. But would take that over both of them dying.

Mara grinned at her, nothing friendly about the expression. "Oh, he bought it. Just got word. Your boyfriend was so distraught it took him twenty minutes to pull himself together, but now he's on his way. To arrest you."

Hayley pulled violently on the handcuffs holding her wrists, wanting desperately to get out of this chair and throw Mara across the room. Mara just laughed.

Mara read another text. "Joshua says Bennett is in 'full agent mode.'"

Of course he was. He wouldn't let the fact that they had a history, or even that she was the mother of his child, stop him if they'd convinced him she was guilty of treason.

"You know what I think sealed the deal?" Mara walked closer, still smiling. "I think it was the fake DNA and blood records we showed Bennett of your son. Records that showed the kid and he had no blood relation whatsoever."

Hayley kicked out with her leg hoping to catch Mara, but she just stepped back.

"So it is true! Ha! That was just a lucky guess on my part, thinking the kid might be his, since I couldn't find any record of you ever dating anyone else, even in the years you were both at different colleges. But I can just imagine handsome Agent Bennett's face when he found out little Mason wasn't his."

Hayley wilted in the chair, the last of her hope deflating. It wouldn't have taken much for them to falsify a medical record for Mason. Unless Cain took the time to truly authenticate it—which he clearly hadn't if he was on his way here—then it would look like Hayley had lied to him about their son.

Just another lie he thought she told him.

He probably couldn't wait to get here to arrest her.

Hayley just stared out the window at the offices across the street. Even if she could get up and wave her arms they probably wouldn't notice her. This building was fully empty, but that one had looked pretty deserted, also.

But trying to figure out a way to get the attention of people who may or may not be across the street was better than sitting here waiting for Cain to arrive and the mistrust between them to sign both of their death warrants.

When she heard the elevator ding she knew it was too late.

Mara came to stand right behind Hayley, her gun pointed directly at her temple. Cain would realize he'd been fooled, but he wouldn't be able to do anything about it.

The door opened and a young man walked in with Cain right in front of him. She could see shock blan-

ket his features as he took in the situation. When he
turned to face the man behind him, the guy had already pulled out his own weapon and had it pointed
at Cain.

The man gestured to Cain's shoulder holster with
his gun. "Take your weapon out, very slowly. Put
it on the ground. If you try any daring heroics I'm
going to be forced to shoot you and Mara will shoot
Hayley."

Cain's eyes narrowed to slits but he did what the
other man asked, putting his gun on the ground and
sliding it away with his foot.

"What the hell is going on, Lawson?"

The man laughed. "Oh sorry, there's been a
change of plans. We don't really need you here to
arrest Hayley. We needed you here so we could make
it look like you were *going* to arrest Hayley and then
the two of you killed each other in the process."

Hayley watched as realization dawned on Cain's
face.

"All that stuff you told me at Omega headquarters…"

"Yeah." Lawson shook his head ruefully. "False.
Ends up your girl is not the only person good with
the computer."

"You made all of it up?"

Lawson shrugged. "No. We did what any good
con man does. We took elements of the truth and
blended them with what we needed them to say."

Hayley had never seen Cain look so defeated. It

crushed something inside her. She pulled at her hand-cuffs again. Cain looked over at them.

"You're the lady who worked at the Bluewater. You were there the night of the fire," he said to Mara.

"We tried to get rid of her that night, but you were too quick. Got her out of the building."

Cain took a few steps toward them, his hand held out almost as an apology to Hayley.

"And the hotel?" he asked. "Someone really was trying to kill Hayley. She didn't set that up."

"Ms. Green has proven exceptionally difficult to kill," Lawson answered. "Unlike her other hacker cohorts, who we were able to eliminate so easily."

Mara pushed at the back of Hayley's head with her gun. "We thought we had more time with you since you were actually following the rules of your parole and not accessing any computers. FYI, your fellow cocriminals accessed them as soon as they could manage it."

Hayley turned her head so she could look at Mara. "So you killed them because you couldn't figure out which one of us had set that trapdoor inside the CET system."

Cain took another few steps toward the window. Maybe he was thinking, like Hayley had, that there was someone across the street he could try to signal. Hayley needed to keep Mara's and Lawson's attention on her.

"We knew it had to be one of the top tier." Lawson followed Cain, keeping his gun pointed at him.

"Some of the hackers weren't capable of that sort of maneuver. Mara never thought it was you, but I did." The man leered at her and Hayley couldn't help but cringe.

"You accessing a computer came at a very inconvenient time. We've made millions in our sales, but our biggest one yet is scheduled for next week," Mara said. "Normally we would just lie low for a few years, let this all blow over. But that sale is too big."

Lawson pushed Cain in the back with his gun. "In the billions with a *b* not an *m*. So even though this is going to bring down some definite heat on the situation, we still had to get rid of both of you. Because we know whatever you know, Hayley, you've told Agent Bennett here."

"You won't hurt Mason?" Hayley didn't even want to bring up her son, but if Cain was going to make a move she wanted to give him every opportunity she could.

Mara tsked at her. "We are not monsters. The baby doesn't have anything to do with this."

"Great." Cain rolled his eyes. "Criminals with a conscience. What is it you're going to sell with your billion-dollar sale? Is that going to cost any lives?"

Lawson just shrugged. "You mean plans for the newest stealth drones? Yeah, I'm sure that's going to come back to cost a few lives. But we're not actually pulling the trigger on those like we would be with the kid."

Cain took another step toward the window.

"Just in case you're thinking you might get someone's attention from the other building, we made sure that was empty, too." Lawson gave them both a big grin.

Hayley deflated into her chair. That had been her last hope, that someone across the street would at least see what was going on, even if they couldn't stop it.

They were going to die here. Her eyes met Cain's. There was so much she wanted to say to him. Even to tell him that she understood how he could've believed the proof they'd given about her guilt. She would never expect him to trust her when what seemed like cold, hard facts of her guilt were laid out in front of him.

She wished she could just hold him one last time. Kiss him. But she knew they weren't going to let her, so she wasn't even going to ask.

Maybe she could take out Mara if they unshackled her before killing her. Hayley had no doubt Cain could disarm Lawson. It was Mara's gun at Hayley's head that was holding him back.

Hayley tried to get Cain's attention without the other two people seeing, to give him some sort of signal to take out the woman. Maybe Hayley would die, but it was better than both of them dying. It was at least a chance.

"Let's get this over with," Mara said to Lawson. "I'm sure the Omega people will be looking for these two soon."

Cain walked all the way over to the window to look out. "Is the senator even in on this at all?"

Both Mara and Lawson laughed. "No. His computers are, but the man himself has nothing to do with it," Mara scoffed. "Although he gave us the perfect platform, didn't he?"

"To be the most vocal opponent of the CET because of the danger of it being hacked? And he really helped us out by making sure all you hackers went to prison so quickly and for so long. Gave us time to figure out who might be onto us." Lawson walked over and picked up Cain's gun from near the door.

Hayley shook her head. "The funny thing is I had just realized that since you'd found the trapdoor I wasn't going to be able to prove anything. We thought it was the senator himself committing the crimes, but would never be able to prove it unless he made a mistake."

Mara reached down and unbuckled one of Hayley's wrists. "Sorry. We couldn't take the chance. Although, had we known that, we might've given you a few more months to live."

"Especially since you're a fugitive," Lawson said. "We could've just let the law do our dirty work for us."

Cain turned from the window as Mara unshackled Hayley's other wrist. Now both of them kept their weapons pointed directly at Hayley's and Cain's heads.

"So let me make sure I understand this," Cain said, shoulders drooping more than Hayley had ever seen them. "You almost killed Hayley in the fire, then hacked law enforcement computers to make it look like she violated her parole, put a contract out on her life, which almost got her killed first by Officer Brickman, then again at the hotel. You kidnapped Hayley, then falsified documents again to make me think Hayley was behind all of this. And then you planned to kill us both."

Lawson looked over at Mara, chuckling. "Damn, it reads like a grocery list of badassery, doesn't it?"

Mara laughed, too. "And don't forget making billions of dollars selling classified documents. I think that should top the list."

Cain glared at her. "I do, too."

"And now we're going to make it look like you two killed each other in an arrest gone wrong." Mara pushed Hayley over toward the windows. "You both have got to have gunpowder residue on your hands for this to be believable for forensic purposes. We know enough to know that."

Hayley tried to catch Cain's eye as Mara put a gun in her hand. Maybe he could dive to the side or something.

Anything.

Finally he looked at her. But instead of trying to communicate, he just winked.

Winked.

What the hell?

"Ready?" Cain said.

Was he talking to her? Was she ready to shoot him? Ready to run? Dive? What was he saying?

Even Lawson was looking at him funny.

"Now," Cain said.

The word was barely out of his mouth before the glass of the window shattered and Hayley screamed, covering her face before she felt arms come around her and she fell to the ground.

Seconds later she peeked up as half a dozen people with guns and full tactical gear stormed into the deserted office. Mara and Lawson were both moaning on the ground, shot but alive.

Cain was lying over her, his body protecting her with his own, his arms covering her head.

"Are you okay?" he asked.

She realized she was. Except for a few cuts from the glass, she was uninjured.

"Yes. Wh-what just happened?"

"Cain, you bastard," someone on the SWAT team called out from across the room after they made sure it was secure. "You got them to admit to every damn thing. That was unbelievable."

Cain sat up and began carefully brushing pieces of glass off her and then himself, ignoring the SWAT team who were now handcuffing Mara and Lawson.

"How did they get here?" Hayley asked, pointing at the SWAT team, still trying to process what had just happened. "Were you able to signal them in some way? Did the team track your cell phone?"

But if so, why would he have *winked* at her just before Mara and Lawson were taken down?

Cain pulled a tiny earpiece out of his ear and showed it to her. "They've been with us the whole time. I was trying to buy them time to get set up and to see what we could get those two—" he gestured toward the criminals, who were now being treated for their gunshot wounds until the ambulance arrived "—to admit. Which, as it turns out, was pretty much everything."

Hayley felt like she was in some sort of daze. Couldn't quite figure out what was going on.

"But he showed you proof that I was selling the secrets."

"Yep. Pretty impressive proof, too."

"If you believed him, then why would you have SWAT here with you?"

Cain reached up and picked a small piece of glass out of her hair, then scooted closer so they were almost chest to chest.

"I never believed for one single second that you were the one committing the treason," he said, running the backs of his fingers down her cheek. "People were *dying* due to the secrets being sold. I knew you would never do that. It didn't matter how many printouts showed me otherwise."

"But what about the DNA testing with Mason?"

Cain rolled his eyes. "At that point I was just trying to keep from pummeling Lawson into the ground. I didn't even so much as read that piece of fiction.

Not to mention a certain birthmark that had sealed the truth for me from the first time I saw Mason."

"So the time Lawson said you needed to pull yourself together?"

Cain's lips brushed against hers. "Time needed to get the *team* together. I knew this would be our best chance to end this once and for all. You're safe now. No one will ever be coming after you or Mason."

Hayley felt a tear leak out from the corner of her eye. She couldn't help it.

"Hey," he said, catching it with his fingertip. "It all worked out. Don't cry."

She wasn't crying because of what had happened all around her.

"You trusted me." Even when presented with overwhelming evidence of why he shouldn't. And they were alive because of it.

He pulled her closer. "You're worth trusting. And I hope I can convince you I'm worth trusting, too. The past is past. You and Mason are my future."

She launched herself into his arms, trying to find words, but having to settle for clinging to him instead. His arms folded around her, arms she knew would keep her safe, lend her strength, protect her and Mason from anything that would attempt to harm them. She would do the same for Cain.

She pulled him closer, desperate to feel him against her. Then suddenly the words she needed to say were so clear. Had been since they were teenagers.

"I love you," she whispered.

He kissed her with a reverence that brought tears back to her eyes.

"Me, too. Always have," he murmured. "Always will."

Chapter Twenty-Three

One month later, Hayley stood back before Judge Nicolaides in his Georgia courtroom. Brandon Han, Omega Sector agent and fully licensed attorney, sat at her side as representation.

Although this time she really shouldn't need it. She'd already been cleared of the fugitive charges, the correct information placed back in the law enforcement computer system. This was to revisit her parole.

Cain sat in the row immediately behind Hayley's table. Ariel had Mason outside in the hall running around.

"I'm glad to see you back here unharmed," the judge said from his seat. "And I understand there's been a change in some of your circumstances? Particularly in your last name?"

Hayley glanced over at Brandon, who just held out his hand for her to answer. After the last two times she'd gone before a judge, Cain could understand her nervousness.

"Yes, your honor. My full name is now Hayley Green Bennett."

"Did your husband ever tell you about the time he burst into my chambers and almost got himself arrested?"

Hayley spun around to him before returning to face the judge. "No, Your Honor."

"No matter. I forgave him seeing as I was once a big high school football fan." Judge Nicolaides looked down at the papers on his desk. "Interesting to me that the arresting officer in your original case was also named Cain Bennett."

"Yes, Your Honor."

Cain could tell Hayley was getting a little nervous.

"Ah, well, if you can get past being married to a man with the same name as your arresting officer, then I guess that's all that matters." The judge's smile said he knew exactly what was going on.

"Yes, sir," Hayley said softly. "I think I can manage."

"What I have in front of me is a petition for the complete repeal of your parole conditions. That, according to multiple agents in federal law enforcement, you have provided critical assistance in stopping terrorists from selling state secrets."

Both of whom would be spending their lives in prison if they didn't end up getting the death penalty. Mara and Lawson had been more than willing to provide details about their upcoming "billions with a *b*" deal in order to get whatever leverage they could for themselves, which hadn't been much.

Hayley nodded. "Yes, Your Honor."

"I trust that any hacking you do in the future will be on behalf of the United States government, not for any nefarious purposes of your own?"

"Your Honor, I am out of the hacking business altogether. I'd like to take the next few years and just concentrate on being a wife and mother."

Judge Nicolaides chuckled. "A job not without its own risks."

"And its own rewards."

The judge nodded. "I once assisted your husband because I told him I was there when he led the high school team to the state championships." He smiled at Hayley. "I was also there long after the hoopla died down and there were very few people left in the stands. You were one of them, waiting for Agent Bennett, very much out of the limelight. He came up to you and wrapped his arms around you like you were his lifeline. I've never forgotten that."

Cain had never forgotten that, either. Everyone had been running around the locker room and school, celebrating, making plans for the victory party. All Cain wanted to do was get to Hayley, who had never been comfortable around crowds or as the center of attention. When he saw her in the stands waiting for him, he'd felt relief, more, course through his whole body.

He had no idea how he'd let something as precious as Hayley get away from him, but he knew he'd never make that same mistake twice.

Judge Nicolaides looked at Cain and then back at Hayley. "Hayley Green Bennett, you are hereby released from the previous conditions of your parole. According to the State of Georgia, all time for your previous crimes has been served and you are free to go with no restrictions." The judge brought his gavel down on his desk. Everyone stood as the judge turned to exit.

Brandon hugged Hayley. "That's it, it's all over."

Cain saw the judge hand something to the bailiff before finding himself wrapped in Hayley's arms. He squeezed her to him in a way that left no room for either of them to doubt his joy in this outcome.

"It's time to move on to today's important events, like getting some ice cream," he whispered.

Her smile was radiant. Breathtaking. "No kidding. Mason will have our heads if we don't get him there soon."

The bailiff walked over and handed a small postcard to Hayley.

"Judge Nicolaides asked me to give this to you and Agent Bennett."

Cain looked up at the judge's bench, but he'd already retired to his chambers.

Hayley turned the card over so they could read it. It was a quote from Zig Ziglar.

We cannot start over, but we can begin now, and make a new ending.

Cain wrapped his arm around Hayley as they walked out the door. Omega Sector would continue their search for the person behind the manifesto and threat of attack, and he would help. But Hayley, like she'd said, was just going to spend as much time as she wanted being a wife and mother. If that was forever, that was fine with him.

They both were free to begin their new—and perfect—ending.

* * * * *

Look for the next book in
USA TODAY *bestselling author Janie Crouch's*
OMEGA SECTOR: UNDER SIEGE *miniseries,*
ARMED RESPONSE, available next month.

And don't miss the previous titles in the
OMEGA SECTOR: UNDER SIEGE *series:*

DADDY DEFENDER
PROTECTOR'S INSTINCT
CEASE FIRE

Available now from Harlequin Intrigue!

Get 4 FREE REWARDS!

We'll send you 2 FREE Books plus 2 FREE Mystery Gifts.

Harlequin® Intrigue books feature heroes and heroines that confront and survive danger while finding themselves irresistibly drawn to one another.

FREE Value Over **$20**

HI18

She couldn't see the bastard behind her but knew he was
waiting. Waiting to watch her die as her strength gave out
and she couldn't support herself anymore.

She tried to yell—even if someone came rushing into the
room, it wasn't going to do much more damage than her
swaying here until her strength gave out—but the sound was
cut off by the rope over her vocal cords. If she wanted to
yell, she was going to have to use one hand to pull the rope
away from the front of her throat. That meant supporting all
her weight with one arm.

Her muscles were already straining from the constant
state of pulling up. Supporting her weight with one arm
wasn't going to work.

But she'd be damned if she was just going to die in front
of this bastard.

She swung her legs up, trying to catch the upper part of the rope, but failed again. Even if she could get her legs hooked up there, she wasn't going to be able to get herself released.

She heard a low chuckle to her side. Bastard. He was enjoying this.

And then the alarm started blaring.

Masked Man muttered a curse and took off up the stairs. Lillian felt her arms begin to shake as the exhaustion from holding her own weight began to take its toll. If it wasn't for the rigorous SWAT training, she'd already be dead.

But even training wouldn't be enough. Physics would win. Her arms began to tremble more and she was forced to let go of the rope to give them a break.

Immediately the rope cut off all oxygen.

When everything began to go black, she reached up and grabbed the rope again. It wasn't long before the tremors took over.

She didn't want to go out like this. Wished she hadn't squandered this second chance she'd had with Jace in her life.

But even thinking of Jace, with his gorgeous blue eyes and cocky grin that still did things to her heart after all these years, couldn't give her any more strength.

She reached back up with her arms and found them collapsing before she even took her weight. Then the noose tightened and jerked around her neck, pulling her body forward, all air gone.

Blackness.

Will Jace and the team get there in time to rescue her? Find out when USA TODAY *bestselling author Janie Crouch's* ARMED RESPONSE *goes on sale August 2018.*
Look for it wherever Harlequin® Intrigue books are sold!

*An engagement of convenience might be the only thing
that can save his family's ranch, but Lucian Granger's
sudden attraction to his bride-to-be, Karlee O'Malley,
will change everything he thought he knew about love...*

*Enjoy a sneak peek at THE LAST RODEO,
part of the **A WRANGLER'S CREEK NOVEL** series
by USA TODAY bestselling author Delores Fossen.*

Karlee walked out onto the ground of the barn where
Lucian had busted his butt eighteen times while competing
in the rodeo. Perhaps he saw this party as a metaphorical
toss from a bronc, but if so, there was no trace of that in his
expression. He smiled, his gaze sliding over her, making
her thankful she'd opted for a curve-hugging dress and the
shoes.

Lucian walked toward her, and the moment he reached
her, he curved his arm around her waist, pulled her to him.

And he kissed her.

The world dissolved. That included the ground beneath
her feet and every bone in her body. This wasn't like the
other stiff kiss in his office. Heck, this wasn't like any other
kiss that'd happened—ever.

The feel of him raced through Karlee, and what damage
the lip-lock didn't do, his scent finished off. Leather and
cowboy. A heady mix when paired with his mouth that she
was certain could be classified as one of the deadly sins.

She heard the crowd erupt into pockets of cheers, but
all of that noise faded. The only thing was the soft sound

of pleasure she made. Lucian made a sound, too. A manly grunt. It went well with that manly grip he had on her and his manly taste. Jameson whiskey and sex. Of course, that sex taste might be speculation on her part since the kiss immediately gave her many, many sexual thoughts.

Lucian eased back from her. "You did good," he whispered.

That dashed the sex thoughts. It dashed a lot of things because it was a reminder that this was all for show. But Lucian didn't move away from her after saying that. He just stood there, looking down at her with those scorcher blue eyes.

"You did good, too," Karlee told him because she didn't know what else to say.

He still didn't back away despite the fact the applause and cheers had died down and the crowd was clearly waiting for something else to happen. Karlee was waiting, as well. Then it happened.

Lucian kissed her again.

This time, though, it wasn't that intense smooch. He just brushed his mouth over hers. Barely a touch but somehow making it the most memorable kiss in the history of kisses. Ditto for the long, lingering look he gave her afterward.

"That was from me," he said, as if that clarified things. It didn't. It left Karlee feeling even more aroused. And confused.

What the heck did that mean?

Will this pretend engagement lead to happily-ever-after?

Find out in THE LAST RODEO
by USA TODAY *bestselling author Delores Fossen,*
available now.

www.Harlequin.com